'You can't run a hospital with no water supply!' Kerrie was appalled at the atmosphere of decay, of nobody caring.

'Oh, there is a supply. Han tends to turn it off at the mains to save it.' Leon put his head in his hands. His white shirt had gathered a coating of dust, and the dust from his hands was transferred to his forehead. Suddenly the big man, the consultant whom everyone feared and obeyed in Tajul, was weary, at a loss, and Kerrie felt a surge of pity towards him.

'You've put dust on your face.' She stood beside him to show him the marks, took his handkerchief from him to wipe them off. His face was turned up to her. She didn't know how it happened, but their faces moved closer together, and suddenly they were kissing each other.

Lancashire born, Jenny Anne read English at Birmingham, returning thence with a BA and RA—the latter being rheumatoid arthritis, which after barrels of various pills, and three operations, led to her becoming almost bionic, with two man-made joints. Married to a junior surgeon in Scotland, who was born in Malaysia, she returned to Liverpool with three Scottish children when her husband went into general practice in 1966. She has written non-stop since then—articles, short stories and radio talks. Her novels just had to be set in a medical environment, which she considers compassionate, fascinating and completely rewarding.

Previous Titles

CARIBBEAN TEMPTATION
MISPLACED LOYALTY

FROM SHADOW
TO SUNLIGHT

BY
JENNY ASHE

MILLS & BOON LIMITED
ETON HOUSE   18–24 PARADISE ROAD
RICHMOND   SURREY   TW9 1SR

First published in Great Britain 1991
by Mills & Boon Limited

© Jenny Ashe 1991

Australian copyright 1991
Philippine copyright 1991
This edition 1991

ISBN 0 263 77383 3

Set in 10½ on 12 pt Linotron Times
03-9109-50721
Typeset in Great Britain by Centracet, Cambridge
Made and printed in Great Britain

CHAPTER ONE

'KERRIE SNOW, you've forgotten the ice-box!'

She was ahead of them, knowing she was late, and the other nurses were teasing her. They had all forgotten the ice-box, after their picnic on the silver sand of Moriba beach, and with feet caked in wet sand, hair tousled, and limbs pleasantly weary, they were all in a hurry to be on duty at six. Kerrie was the only English girl on the staff of the Sultan Ali Tabatabai Klinik, and the Malay girls were still getting used to her name. They pronounced it 'Ke Ris No' because they thought it sounded more oriental—then they would laugh in their high tinkling voices because they said it was pretty. They had made her feel at home right from the start, especially Kim.

'We all forgot the box!' she laughed. 'But you go on—I'll get it. *Baiklah*! Sister won't be cross with me.' She was senior staff nurse, and next in seniority to Sister Chan. She didn't mind going back—they were a good-natured lot, and she was grateful to them. Malaysia had been the ideal antidote to the shock of the sudden break-up of her engagement— she had even chosen her wedding-dress. Philip's announcement, out of the blue, that he wanted to end the relationship hurt Kerrie less now that she was in a new and exciting environment. The sun shone down so benignly, the palm trees towered into the deep blue so elegantly, and the shimmering beauty of the South China Sea stretched to a magic horizon. She had been right to come. The challenge of a new hospital, a new country, had given her much less time to brood. Now when she thought of Philip, he belonged to her other world, and eight thousand miles created a barrier between herself and her heartbreak.

She wrapped her yellow *pareo* round her waist, hiding the slim sandy legs that were already getting a tan. Completely oblivious to her own fair good looks, she hitched up the straps of her spotted bikini top and ran back to the grassy picnic area beneath the coconut palms at the edge of the sand, where they had been drinking their iced cola, and eating curry puffs, and delicious cashew nuts that grew in the next village along the coast, and were roasted by drying them in the hot sun.

Then Kerrie stopped, gasped, and put back the blonde hair from her eyes, caught completely unawares. A tall man, dressed in brief black swimming-trunks, was holding her ice-box out of the way, while his pretty companion draped a batik cloth on the ground and placed her own picnic basket on it.

The woman was beautiful—with honey-coloured skin, cleverly made-up almond eyes, blue-black hair piled in a glossy chignon, and decorated with a delicate white hibiscus flower. Kerrie might have stared at her if the tall man had been less striking. But he had already made his impression, and Kerrie stood as though she had been stunned by a heavy blow. Could an ordinary mortal be so perfect? She had seen good-looking men in Hollywood films, but always believed they wore make-up. Surely no one could be so completely desirable without even trying? Long straight legs, the figure of a male model, the muscles of an athlete—and those black eyes, half hidden under straight black brows. Direct, challenging and totally dominating. Kerrie stood, her voice vanished, and only her eyes spoke.

The man turned at the rustle her feet made in the grass, and his proud mouth curled into a smile, totally altering the dominant image that those fierce eyes had proclaimed. 'This must be yours?' He spoke in accented English, and held out the ice-box. Kerrie couldn't help noticing how the muscles in his arm and shoulder caught the sunlight, smooth and brown and asking to be touched.

Touched? How could she even think such a thing? Blushing, she nodded. 'Thank you—*terimakasih*. I left it behind. I—I——' For goodness' sake! She had been an engaged woman only a month or so ago. She knew what it felt like to desire a man. Yet she had never experienced such a violent physical attraction towards anyone before. She backed away. 'I'm sorry——'

His voice was purring, amused and kind. 'Shall I carry it for you?'

'No, thank you. I'm. . .fine, thank you——' Kerrie turned, her cheeks flaming, and ran into the trees to hide her embarrassment. She hoped that the woman hadn't noticed her discomfort. Lucky lady, to have such a man. A man to worship, to cherish, to yield to, delight in. Kerrie paused in the shadows, the fronded palm leaves dappling the sand. She waited, smoothing back her untidy hair with shaking hands, until her breathing was normal, before she made her way to the path that led to the back door of the nurses' home behind the main *klinik*.

She spoke to herself as she dusted off the sand, rinsed her face, and changed quickly into her uniform. 'You made a bit of a fool of yourself there, my girl. It's quite normal for a woman to be physically attracted to a good-looking man. It's only hormones doing their job. What a good thing you probably won't see him again—a man like that could become quite an obsession if you saw him every day.'

She had no time to wash her hair, so she brushed it as vigorously as she could, to get the sand out, before pinning on the rather old-fashioned little white lace cap. It was lucky, really, that duty called. She could try to forget about that man, about his piercing eyes and his rounded muscles, his briefest of brief trunks and the thrusting thighs with their covering of downy dark hairs. . .

Sister Chan brought her down to earth. 'Madame Karela wants you to bath her, Staff Nurse. And after that Mr Singh needs someone to help him with his speech therapy.'

'But, Sister——'

'Yes, I do know that bathing should be done by the junior staff, and that Mr Singh should wait for the therapist. Why must you always argue with me, Staff Nurse? When I give an order I expect it to be obeyed at once. Both these patients have asked specifically for you. When patients are paying as much as they do here, Staff, we try to comply with their requests.'

Kerrie tried to control her expression, but Sister saw it. Sour-faced and thin, she said, 'And the sooner you forget your British training the better. Money talks here, and no one tries to pretend it doesn't. You think you had equality according to need, I'm sure. But if you think about it, you didn't get wealthy people staying in Government hospitals, did you?'

'Quite a few, actually.' But Kerrie spoke gently, not wanting to provoke yet another argument with her starchy sister. Kerrie had her own ideas about Sister Chan. Crossed in love—that was the first one. Kerrie Snow knew a bit about how that felt. Brought up in an unloving home was the next. Or maybe she was sickening for an ulcer. They could all account for Sister Chan's unbending emphasis on efficiency, the total lack of smiles, and the strained, though almost unreadable look in her narrow black eyes.

'Madame Karela, good evening.' As soon as Kerrie entered the elegantly furnished room, with its cool white counterpane, lace curtains and smooth champagne-coloured carpet, she forgot that the woman in the satin-covered bed was a millionairess, and instead saw her only as a pathetic little figure, whose growth had been operated on before Kerrie came to the Sultan. Professor da Cruz had done his best, and he was an eminent surgeon. This thin, pale relic of a woman in her expensive silken nightdress had once been a vital person, running her own businesses, with dozens of employees at her beck and call. And now all that could help her was pity and compassion. She turned her large sunken eyes towards Kerrie, who said gently, 'You'd like me to see to your bath?'

The voice was hushed and apologetic. 'You were so gentle last time. Do you mind very much?'

'No, of course I don't mind. Why did I come into nursing? Here to help, Madame Karela. I'll be as quick as I can, then you can rest.'

'Thank you, Nurse Snow. I feel at ease with you.' The skin over the high cheekbones was taut and papery, the eyes strangely bright in their gaunt hollows. The least Kerrie could do was try to make her suffering less. The woman went on, 'Professor da Cruz told me he had removed the tumour completely. It is up to me now to get well.'

Kerrie brought the bowl of warm water and took *madame*'s luxury soap and flannel from her cupboard. She put on her most encouraging look. She had learnt early how to hide the truth from patients, how to smile and help them feel that everything was all right. 'And I know you will! Now, I'll do my best not to hurt you, but you realise how important it is to maintain total asepsis over the wound area. I'm afraid I have to wipe every inch.'

The little lady smiled, although her forehead was wrinkled with fear. Her teeth were perfect, and the etched lines formed by the smile emphasised the thinness of her skin. 'I once thought no one could understand pain unless they had experienced it, Nurse, yet you seem to. You have such pity in your hands. If I couldn't see for myself how young and fit you are, I'd swear you had known pain.'

'No, *madame*. Only a sprained ankle once on the hockey field at school. That was enough for me!'

Kerrie chattered, to take the patient's mind off what she was doing. She had washed *madame*'s arms and legs, and now she uncovered the dressing over the wound. The shrunken stomach sagged, revealing sharp hipbones and ribs. The eight-inch scar was still livid, the stitches puckering the skin. Kerrie held back her pity, and concentrated on being as gentle as possible.

Madame Karela said suddenly, in her quiet, calm voice, 'Maybe you have known pain in the heart, Nurse? That can be just as bad as this, you know.'

Kerrie's fingers involuntarily squeezed the flannel over the bowl, at her patient's accurate diagnosis of her life story. She turned from the mechanics of her work to look into Madame Karela's face. For a moment the patient became the doctor, as Kerrie confessed. 'I expect you guessed I had to have a reason for coming out to Malaysia to work? My fiancé decided to marry someone else. It was a shock, coming as it did after the wedding invitations had been sent out. But it's over now. I've forgotten about him.'

'You don't forget the pain, though?'

Kerrie forced a laugh. 'Now I know why you're such a successful businesswoman, *madame*! You can read minds!'

As she put the things away, her patient said, 'I do hope there's someone else for you soon, my dear.'

Kerrie laughed again, and, bending down, she whispered, 'Don't tell anyone, *madame*, but I met the man of my dreams today. Pity I forgot to ask him his name!' She straightened up and said, 'Seriously, *madame*, I'd rather not get involved again. Feelings are very fragile things, and I don't want to be hurt like that again. I suppose, in a way, I feel I won't ever be able to trust a man enough to allow him to get close. I just want to make a satisfying career here. The Sultan is a splendid place to work, and the nurses have such a good time, being close to the beach, and to the town. It's just like a holiday. I couldn't bear to spoil it by falling in love again.'

Madame leaned back on her satin pillows, and the bright eyes were wise. 'You'll meet him again, Nurse, I'm sure of it. The man of your dreams, *lah*? Lucky girl!'

Kerrie stood for a moment, eyes misting a little at the memory of the ideal man she had looked at for a moment, hardly believing anyone could be so perfect. And then she had blown everything away by acting like a tongue-tied idiot. Just as well, really, remembering her decision not to get romantically involved. Men were to be treated with caution from now on. A slight smile lifted the corners of her mouth as she recalled the aristocratic beauty of his face. He could have been a sultan. . .

She heard the door open, and Sister Chan was chiding again. How very predictable! 'You're taking a long time, Staff.'

Madame Karela said quickly, 'Oh, no, she has only just finished. She's a precious commodity, Sister—a nurse who can be kind and gentle as well as thorough.'

'I'm so sorry, *madame*.' Sister Chan's lips narrowed. 'But you understand—this wing is full, and there's so much to do. Come when you're ready, Staff Nurse Snow.'

And Kerry said mildly, but with a hint of steel, 'Did you think I wouldn't, Sister?' She smiled her thanks to *madame* and followed Sister Chan down the flower-decked corridor.

Back in the office, Sister snapped, 'That was rude and uncalled-for, Staff. I'm getting tired of your uppity ways. A UK training doesn't excuse bad manners.' And, when Kerrie tried to explain, she went on quickly, 'Oh, go and see to Mr Singh! Right away, please.'

'Right away.'

'And later you can perhaps explain why you were late coming on duty.'

'I had to go back for something we forgot.'

Sister Chan's tone relaxed slightly. 'Was Professor da Cruz down at the beach? He came back this morning, and I think he went down for a swim before starting back at work.' She appeared to have a soft spot for the professor. Her stern face mellowed, and her mouth lost its hard narrow look.

Kerrie had assumed the Professor would be old—definitely white-haired, unless he was bald. 'I'm afraid I've never met Professor da Cruz. I don't know what he looks like. He'd just finished his session of operations here when I came.'

'Of course—I forgot. He has been operating at one of his other hospitals. But he's definitely back now. He popped in to let me know that he's coming in this evening, I think. That's why I want the entire wing to be spick and span for him. He'll be at the Sultan for the next three months now. Better go

along and try to make some progress with Mr Singh's
speech.'

'Yes, Sister.'

Mr Singh was a jolly man of about sixty-five. He
laughed a lot at his own misfortune, and made his
visiting relatives, of whom he had a horde, smile as
well, through their tears. Kerrie too felt sorry,
because his stroke had annihilated his speech. His
ideas were still there, but he had no way of express-
ing them. Even his right hand was useless. Kerrie
felt her own eyes fill, as she watched him trying to
make himself understood. He had been a school-
master. Now he was a pupil again, and frustrated
with his own inability to communicate.

She pulled up a chair and sat beside him. 'You
have to try to be an absolutely brilliant patient, Mr
Singh! I know how it must feel. The therapist has
assured us that progress will be made—only it will
be in weeks, rather than minutes, so don't expect
instant miracles. Can you do that?'

He nodded, with an attempt at the lop-sided
smile. Then, with his left hand, he scrawled on a pad
that hung round his neck, over his crimson silk
pyjamas. Kerrie deciphered the spidery words.
'Schoolboy again!'

She nodded, and smiled. 'I'll try to be a kind
headmistress.'

He laughed at that, and wrote, 'No caning,
please.'

She smoothed her pale blue uniform over her
knees and took the exercise book with the lessons
he was supposed to be practising. Simple words,
they were, designed to re-train the brain to work in

conjunction with his mouth and voice. Very slow
she pronounced the words with him, emphasising
the shape his lips ought to take, and the part of the
mouth where he had to form his consonants.

There came voices from the corridor, but Kerrie
went on working with her patient. Sister Chan was
coming—probably wanting to give her more menial
tasks, as a way of keeping her in her place. She
didn't mind. She was used to Chan now. And
anyway, as she had told Madame Karela, the other
girls were nice, the hours of work reasonable, and
the beach only minutes away. Working at the Sultan
was hardly like working at all. One crosspatch of a
sister couldn't spoil things for Kerrie.

Sister Chan was talking to a man. Yes, of course,
it must be old Professor da Cruz, the owner not only
of the Sultan, but three other hospitals besides.
Kerrie pursed her lips as she tried to get Mr Singh
to say 'You', and thought to herself that it was nice
of the professor to call in and see all his patients at
every visit. He must be a pleasant man, for Sister
Chan to go all misty-eyed about him, and for the
other nurses to be looking forward to his return.

Then she froze, and the word she had been saying
somehow didn't come out. Surely she recognised
that purring, velvet voice that was saying behind
her, in a charmingly accented English, 'And this is
our stroke patient, Mr Singh? How are you today,
Mr Singh? I hope you are making sure he gets
intensive physio, Sister.'

'I'll see to it, naturally, sir.' Sister Chan sounded
different—almost cooing with politeness and syrup.
'He's just having speech therapy now.'

'Very wise.' Kerrie imagined Chan preening herself at the compliment. 'A man of your education must get very frustrated at not being able to make yourself understood verbally, Mr Singh.' Kerrie's head was down, her cheeks growing warm, as there was a rustle of white coats, and of Sister opening Mr Singh's case notes. She ventured to turn her head very slightly. It was the same man: tall, keen-eyed, square-jawed. She rose to her feet, with almost a bob of a curtsy, and stood to one side as the aristocratic Professor da Cruz shook hands with the patient, and asked him if he was comfortable.

Da Cruz didn't look directly at Kerrie. She was enormously glad of that, because she felt sure her face must be scarlet—and not with sunburn. 'Thank you, Nurse.' He took her chair, in order to listen to the patient's chest with a slim gold stethoscope. Kerrie heard her own breathing, and wondered if anyone else could. To think this elegant, suave consultant was the same man she had last seen wearing very brief swimming-trunks, and revealing more or less all of the rest of his Greek god's body! She recalled his amused look at her small bikini top and dishevelled hair, as she stumbled over her words, and then fled in disarray. Fortunately the professor didn't seem to connect her, at the moment, with the sandy young urchin at the beach. She began to relax.

He stood straight, and nodded approvingly. Then, looking suddenly into Kerrie's face with those startling eyes, he said quietly, 'Back to the speech therapy, Nurse.'

'Yes, Doctor.' Her voice struggled from a husky throat.

He turned at the door, ushering a gratified Sister Chan out before him, and said directly to Kerrie, 'It might do you both a bit of good! You seem to have a spot of laryngitis.' And he deliberately winked, before closing the door behind his rustling white coat.

Kerrie sank into the chair and closed her eyes in embarrassment. He had recognised her after all. When she opened them, it was to find Mr Singh chuckling at her discomfort. Then he opened his mouth, and a croak came out, followed by words—slow, but recognisable. 'Hand-some, eh?'

Regaining some composure, Kerrie nodded and replied with a laugh, 'A bit younger than I'd imagined him to be.' Then she realised what her patient had done and stared with a broad smile. 'I say, you spoke by yourself! You spoke to me! Well done, Mr Singh—very well done!'

Kerrie never meant to tell anyone about meeting the professor on the beach. It was enough of an embarrassment that he knew and she knew. But the following day off she went to town with her friend Kim Mayang, and, during their chatter, when they stopped for a root beer at a Kentucky Fried Chicken house, she found herself longing to know more about their chief. 'So the professor isn't married, then? I'm surprised. So handsome. I thought he would have been snapped up long ago.'

'Everyone says there was a terribly romantic unhappy episode a long time ago—he wanted to

arry this minor princess, and her parents made her
go to Kashmir to marry into royalty. Bit of a story-
book tragedy, if it's true.'

'Poor chap.'

'Oh, he's OK now—we think he might marry Dr
Nader. She's doing research into diabetic children,
and they've been working together on some project.
They seem to see quite a lot of each other. You
won't have seen her yet—she's still on leave. She's
quite good-looking, for a medic. Bit stand-offish,
though. Naturally everyone thinks she isn't nice
enough for him.'

Kerrie didn't reply at once. Talk of weddings
brought back images of Philip and that other girl
who had lured him away. Her broken heart wasn't
quite healed, then. Kim said, 'Let's go and try
clothes on!'

'I thought you always had your dresses made by a
tailoress?'

'I do—it's cheaper. But how do you know what
suits you unless you try some on?' Kerrie smiled,
and went willingly along with her effervescent
friend.

Later they found a pavement café, and ordered
lemonade. Kerrie noticed a young man in jeans and
a loud checked shirt eyeing them from another table.
Suddenly he came across and put his hand on Kim's
shoulder as though he knew her. 'Where have you
been hiding, love?' He was Australian, that was
sure.

Kim looked up, apparently pleased to see him.
'Hi, Rick. I've been around. Where have you been?'

'Who's your friend?' Rick was scanning Kerrie's

face with interest, and he transferred his hand from Kim's shoulder to shake Kerrie's hand firmly. 'I'm Rick O'Grady. I'm at the Sultan too. Hope to see lots more of you, Kerrie.' He had very blue eyes, and a direct, honest face.

'Join us?' invited Kim.

'Afraid I've got a list in ten minutes. See you two ladies around.'

He was gone, leaving them both slightly breathless. Kerrie said, 'Did I hear right? A list? That means he's a surgeon?'

Kim laughed. 'A very junior one.'

'I thought he looked like a planter. At least something to do with the outdoors.'

'If it were left to him, he'd operate outdoors! He likes wide-open spaces. I don't think he'll stay long at the Sultan. He doesn't get on too well with the prof.'

'Why ever not? He seems nice.'

'Maybe he's a bit too unconventional for Professor da Cruz. And he's rather ambitious.'

'Ambitious?' Kerrie raised her eyebrows. 'What's wrong with that?'

Kim leaned forward. 'It isn't official, but we've heard an uncle in Australia is lending him the money to set up his own hospital, right here in Tajul. The prof thinks it's unethical. They had a blazing row.'

'Gosh!' The handsome consultant suddenly didn't seem quite the paragon Kerrie had first believed. 'That's a bit childish, isn't it? If the Sultan is doing well and giving good value, they shouldn't mind a bit of competition.'

'Theoretically, no. But apparently Rick has been

chatting up some of the staff—nurses and physios, offering them more if they work for him. Poaching, I think the word is. Da Cruz actually suspended Rick for a while, when he first heard. But Rick isn't ready to start his own place yet—he hasn't had enough operating experience.'

'I didn't think doctors acted like children.' Kerrie was feeling slightly disappointed in the professor. The image of him as the ideal man began to crumble.

Later, she was crossing the lawn alone, from the nurses' apartments, when she heard the sound of a car engine, and turned to see a low-slung American car slipping silently to a stop outside the main entrance to the *klinik*. Professor Leon da Cruz stepped out, alone, unfolding long legs from the driving seat. He was wearing a three-piece suit and silk tie. His shirt gleamed white, and his shoes shone like mirrors, reflecting the palm trees above him and the wrought ironwork of the gracious entrance hall.

He's like a sultan himself, thought Kerrie, holding back so that he wouldn't see her coming. Her fascination with the professor had ebbed away slightly. Arrogant and dictatorial—thinks his juniors should obey his whims, and not try and set up their own life. I know whose side I'd be on if he asked me. Why shouldn't Rick—or anyone else—set up on their own if they want to? Handsome as a Greek statue he may be, but, from now on, handsome is as handsome does. I suddenly don't find you quite so attractive, Professor da Cruz. She walked behind him, wishing he hadn't made such an impression on her with his physical presence that afternoon on the beach.

No longer would her heart flutter at his attentions. And he had had the audacity to wink at her, that day in Mr Singh's room! She hoped he wouldn't try that again. She stepped up the three white marble steps—only to find Leon da Cruz standing in the shadows, holding the glass door open for her. She met his gaze calmly, unsmiling. Professor da Cruz gave a slight bow, and his dark eyes were in shadow under those brows, unreadable. 'After you, Nurse.' And he waited while she entered, brushing unavoidably against the fresh newness of his elegant form, smelling of aftershave and soap, and a warm maleness that hit her again in the stomach. Kerrie held her head high, and murmured polite thanks. But she didn't look back.

CHAPTER TWO

'KERRIE, nice to see you again. Uniform suits you.'
Rick's unmistakable Australian brogue boomed
along the corridor of the theatre wing. Kerrie
turned, embarrassed that the compliment could have
been heard in all three theatres and probably the
recovery-room as well. Kim was right—he was much
more suited to an outdoor life.

'Hello, Rick.' She was forced to stop, as he bore
down on her from Theatre Two like a rugby player
about to tackle her. 'How are you?'

He stopped and looked down at her, his eyes
skimming over the outline of her figure with obvious
approval. His shoulders in the surgical gown seemed
to fill the corridor, and she was unable to get past
him. Not that she wanted to—those appreciative
blue eyes reminded her that she had taken a liking
to him at first sight. He said, 'Well now, that's
mighty civil of you to ask. Why don't we discuss it
over dinner some time?'

It was sudden, but she couldn't see any reason
why not. Rick appeared to be as friendly as all the
others, and it would be nice to go out. Kerrie had
been thinking of her broken engagement last night.
Sometimes it still rankled. She had felt herself a
failure—somehow unattractive to men. 'Oh—yes,
thank you.' She would keep it casual. No falling for

22

anyone. Just a friendly date, with someone cheerful and happy-go-lucky.

'Tonight?'

There was something very persuasive in the way he tilted his blond head on one side, and his lips curled up just a little. Maybe he was too sure of himself. But he had a right to be—he was good-looking and apparently a passable surgeon, with a good future in front of him. Rick O'Grady radiated optimism and natural friendliness, and it was irrestibly persuasive to Kerrie, who still nursed the memory of her broken heart. 'Thanks. That would be nice.'

'Pick you up at seven.' He smiled. 'I didn't realise you worked in Theatre. Can't think why we haven't bumped into one another before. *Ciao*, Kerrie, till tonight.'

She knew her cheeks were pink as she walked through the recovery-room. The patients there were in varying stages of somnolence, but the charge nurse was grinning, and so was Kim Mayang. 'Careful, Kerrie,' said Kim. 'I wondered how long it would be before he moved in. He's been through the entire nurses' home, you know, so don't believe any lines he shoots about your being special. You're probably about number fifteen and that's only in the Sultan!'

Kerrie realised that Kim might have been one of that number. She said carefully, 'I do know the type, you know. Not the settling down sort, but they know how to be charming and make good conversation. No harm in that, surely?'

Charge Nurse Jami Arul turned from the patient

he was monitoring. 'You can take care of yourself, Kerrie?'

She looked at him, wondering at his concerned tone. 'Yes, of course I can. I'm twenty-six years old, I was once engaged to be married, and I'm now totally immune to male charm. I know just how untrustworthy men can be. Why the question?'

Jami looked down at the thermometer in his hand and said casually, 'Oh, nothing much. Only one of the nurses christened him the Australian boa-constrictor!'

Kim said quietly, 'Jami means don't go anywhere too private, that's all. Rick's a red-blooded young man.'

'Thanks for the advice.' Kerrie walked away, and her thoughts weren't with the Australian boa-constrictor now, but with Philip Wentworth. She had thought Philip to be something like that—he was a very physical person, and she had thought his need for close contact rather excessive. He had blamed her—told her she was unnatural, even frigid. Yet she felt herself normal, with normal urges. How on earth did one know what was normal? Still, fore-warned, tonight she would make sure Rick O'Grady didn't turn their little dinner into an orgy.

It was difficult to choose something modest to wear, because of the heat of that tropical night. Indoors, there was air-conditioning, but outside it was steamily sultry, and to wear a high neckline would have been uncomfortable. However, Kerrie compromised, with a thin cotton blouse trimmed with lace, which she could leave unbuttoned just at the top. She stood and admired her reflection, pleased with the way the white of the blouse showed off her tanned face, neck and arms. To make the outfit more formal, she chose a straight linen skirt of navy blue. Navy sandals on bare brown feet completed the outfit, and she left her hair loose, curling naturally to her shoulders.

Rick knocked at the door exactly at seven. Opening it, prepared to make it clear that to her he was just another pal, not a threatening sexual male, she said, 'Hello, Rick. I didn't know doctors were ever on time!'

'But you're ready, sweetheart, which is all that matters. You look good enough to eat.'

He wore a short-sleeved shirt, open at the neck, and close-fitting cotton jeans. Again Kerrie thought how little like a typical surgeon he looked. Ignoring his patronising tone, and hoping it was only temporary, she said, 'It's nice to be asked out informally for a change. Thanks.'

His deep voice sounded caring then. 'Seems to be a story behind that, love. You've had a bad experience, maybe? Let's go in search of my favourite grub, and we'll have a heart-to-heart about Life, the Universe and Everything!' And, as he ushered her before him towards the main entrance, he said, 'You know, I haven't ever had a date with an English girl.'

His car was a blue Malaysian Proton. As they drove along the roughly asphalted road parallel to the coastline, Kerrie said, 'I don't think they're any different from other girls.'

'Have you ever been out with an Aussie? Now

they're really different from the rest of the world, honest!'

'You're boasting.'

'Never!'

Kerrie was relieved that Rick O'Grady knew how to be entertaining and amusing. She realised it was something she had missed. He chatted cheerfully, but more about her than himself. He chose a secluded but not too quiet restaurant, jutting out into the sea on stilts, where the fish were still alive in an indoor tank, until chosen by the customers, to be grilled over charcoal. He knew about wine. And though he filled her glass, he didn't encourage her to have more than she wanted. Any fears planted in her mind by Jami and Kim soon vanished, with Rick's gentle, bantering conversation.

'How about a walk along the beach? We can walk all the way back to the Sultan on the sand if you'd like that?'

'But your car?'

'I'll jog back for it—I need the exercise. Only a mile and a half. Want to?'

'I'd love it.' The sound of the waves was gentle, and the night a wonderful clear dark blue, scattered with stars. 'I'll have to take my shoes off.'

'Don't worry, I'll keep my eyes skinned for jelly-fish.' And he led her down some wooden steps, where a couple of high-prowed boats were moored to a small jetty. 'Fishermen. They'll go out in about an hour—just before midnight. Look, you can see a couple already out near the horizon. That's tomorrow's dinner they're after.'

'They look like fallen stars,' exclaimed Kerrie, as

she just descried the two flickering lights that identified the fishermen's tiny boats out on the vast ocean.

She looked up when Rick didn't answer. He was watching her, not the boats. 'You know you're very lovely?' His voice was low and husky, and his eyes were admiring. 'If I were the guy who dumped you, I'd want my head examined.'

'How do you know it was Philip who did the dumping, and not me?'

'You wouldn't look so wistful, love.' Rick took Kerrie's sandals in his hand, and they set off along the warm pale sand towards the Sultan. A slight breeze disturbed the palm fronds above them, making them rustle an accompaniment to the whispering sea. He put his arm loosely around her shoulders. It wasn't a threatening touch, just amicable, as they walked and talked. 'I read it in your eyes,' he said.

'It wouldn't have bothered me if he was just any man. I believe in being free to choose to go out with anyone. But when he'd made a commitment—when the wedding date was fixed—then I think I had a right to resent his behaviour.' Kerrie stopped. She hadn't said so much about her past to anyone in Malaysia. 'I didn't mean to talk about it.'

'I'm glad you did, because I can tell you now that your precious Philip is a prize idiot, and you're well out of that marriage.'

'That's what my mother said.'

'She's right. Don't you see? He must be crazy. To have someone like you devoted to him, and choosing someone else—his judgement is clearly off its trolley. If you'd gone through with that wedding,

Kerrie, love, you'd be regretting it already—I'm sure of it.'

'Are you some sort of expert, Rick?' She said it with a smile, knowing his past history from her friends, and wondering what he was going to say for himself.

His hand gripped her shoulder more tightly, and he stopped and drew her to face him. The starlight made his fair hair look almost white, and his rugged face in the shadows looked strong and comfortable, and not threatening at all. When he kissed her, though it was sudden, it was a gentle, comfortable kiss, with no passion and no undercurrents of uncontrolled desire. He drew away, and kissed the tip of her nose. They were both smiling. Then he turned, and they walked another stretch of sand. Kerrie felt supremely content. Rick said casually, 'I was married oncc.'

'Unhappily?'

'Yeah—a bad mistake. I guess it more or less put me off the idea of what you call commitments.'

'I can see that.' How comforting to have met a man who felt the same as she did about relationships.

'And I've my career to think of. Until I get settled in a permanent job, no way can I settle down.'

'I think that's fairly sensible.'

'Do you, Kerrie? Then that makes you a wise woman. I don't meet too many of them!'

'You make me sound like a grandmother, Rick!'

Kerrie laughed and joked, as she hadn't done for a long time, feeling totally at ease with him. When they reached the path up to the Sultan, she said, 'I'll be OK from here, thanks. And thank you again for a super evening.'

'The pleasure was mine, Kerrie. All mine.' Rick turned to face her. 'What do you think of the boss, Kerrie?'

'The professor? He's all right, I suppose.' She was wary of telling Rick what she knew about him and Professor da Cruz.

'Not wild about him, then?'

'Definitely not remotely wild about him.'

'Sensible girl.' And with another gentle, warm lingering kiss, his arms scarcely holding her, he whispered 'Goodnight,' then turned, and started to run silently along the silvery shore. She watched him for a while. Her first date since—since long ago. Rick O'Grady had all the qualities that might make Philip Wentworth ancient history, and make Professor da Cruz totally irrelevant. . .

They were busy next morning in the Sultan Ali Tabatabai. But Kerrie was well aware of the buzz of interest, as the other girls wondered how she had got on with the hospital Romeo. Their excitement rubbed off on to her, and she found herself smiling at their curious glances and enquiring faces. 'It was just a dinner and a walk along the sand, Kim.'

'He was a gentleman, then?'

'Very much so.'

Slightly disappointed, the other girls' interest ebbed.

But Kim said, 'It was to put you off your guard. Make you relax and trust him. Don't take him at face value.'

'Maybe.'

'Did he make another date?'

'No.'

'Oh.'

Some days later, as Kerrie helped the domestic staff serve the patients' lunches, Sister Chan came up to her and said, 'Leave that, Staff. Professor da Cruz wishes to speak to you. Better hurry.'

She didn't hurry. Why should she? The professor was more or less Rick's enemy, and preventing him from setting up his own *klinik*, possibly preventing him from finding himself a wife and making a home. It just wasn't fair. Kerrie liked Rick, and had no time for dictators. She had also discovered how much the professor charged for operating, and thought he overcharged his patients. Leon da Cruz was now the single thorn in her Malaysian bed of roses. What a good job he wouldn't be here too much longer. He was due to go up-country to another of his hospitals. She knocked on the door of his office. 'Sir? You wanted me.'

There was amusement in the dark eyes as he raised his head from his case-notes, reminding her of the moment when they first met. Again, in spite of herself, Kerrie felt the impact of his stunning looks, his air of total control, and calm authority. What a tragedy that inside that perfect torso was only a petty, small-minded soul. 'Sit down, please. I was watching you in Theatre this week, Nurse Snow.'

She had not know he was there. 'I didn't see you, sir.'

'No. Because you were doing your job so well—

admirably. I wish there were more theatre staff with your ability to read your surgeon's mind.'

It was decent of him to say so. Not many consultants took the trouble. A brief 'Well done' or 'Ta, Staff,' was all she'd usually heard from former colleagues. 'Thank you, sir,' she said politely.

He cleared his throat, and straightened the papers in front of him. 'Now, as you know, I have two other hospitals in this state.'

'Yes, I heard that.'

'I leave tomorrow for an operating session lasting about a week in Kalang Bahru.'

'Yes, sir.'

'You will come with me. The theatre there is very poorly organised, and I need someone competent to get the place up to the standard of the Sultan. I think you are up to the job, Staff Nurse Snow. I'd like you to take it on.'

Go with him? He was her employer, certainly, but a man she found upsetting, a man she intended to stay as far away from as possible. 'Oh, but——'

'Naturally you'll get a salary as administrator, in addition to your nursing pay.'

He looked deep into her eyes to catch her reaction to his offer. Those forbidding eyebrows were again belied by the kindly twinkle in his eyes. She knew very well that the force of his personality was such that she dared not refuse. But it would have been mannerly of him to ask, instead of tell her that she was going. She said, trying not to stammer, 'I—was just getting used to the routine here, sir.'

'Ordinary nursing duties? I would have thought a

girl of your intelligence would enjoy the challenge of reorganising an entire department.'

Honesty won. 'It's true. It would take more than a week, though.'

'As long as you need. Then you agree?'

'I thought it was an order.'

He smiled then, and stood up. Kerrie found her cheeks growing warm again, faced with his powerful physical presence. 'Did I omit to say please?'

Gaining confidence from her determination not to like him, she said, 'You said "You will come with me", sir.'

'My word! I had no intention of sounding like the commandant of a prisoner-of-war camp!'

And, as Kerrie saw the funny side, she couldn't help a stifled chuckle. She hastily looked down at her hands, which were twisting together like a schoolgirl's in front of a headmaster. 'It didn't really sound like that. I think you meant it to sound like a question,' she admitted.

'I did, Kerrie.' How sweet her name sounded, when spoken in that gentle accent. 'What do you say?'

Facing that amount of personality, that amount of charm and knowing very well that he paid her wages and she would be totally out of line to refuse, Kerrie agreed. 'You said tomorrow, sir?'

'Yes. But if you could spare the time to come to my apartment at six, we could have a drink and talk over the details.'

It was another order she couldn't refuse—a drink with the professor. Kerrie made a mental note to say nothing to the girls. Yet she would have to tell them where she was going next morning. She twisted her hands together again, realised she was doing it, and forced herself to stop. 'Six o'clock.' Her mouth felt dry.

'And Kerrie——'

'Yes, sir?'

'One more thing. I wouldn't have too much to do with O'Grady, if I were you.'

She breathed in deeply, her temper rising. 'Doesn't that come under the heading of private life—sir?'

He came round to the front of the desk. His suit was thin sharkskin, and it fitted his figure accurately, following every line of the lithe body. Kerry blushed again, as she recalled what he looked like virtually naked. There was so little of his body she hadn't seen. The power-hammer that had pumped into her solar plexus at their first meeting began to pump again. Professor da Cruz said, 'Not quite. I realise it might look as though I'm interfering. But you're new here, and under my roof, so to speak. I've known Mr O'Grady for some considerable time— you haven't, that's all.'

She stood up, painfully aware that only a foot or so separated their warm bodies, that she had to tilt her head to face his dark, hypnotic gaze. 'I'll bear it in mind, sir.' She turned to go to the door.

'Six o'clock, then.'

'Yes, professor.'

'Thank you.' The purring words, and the smile that went with them, might have been calculated to put Kerrie at her ease. But her heart was beating very noticeably as she made her way back, past the entrance foyer with its tinkling fountain over a pool of lillies and real goldfish, to the nursing wing.

'What did he want?' Sister Chan was nothing if not direct.

'Er—I'm to spend a week or two at Kalang Bahru, apparently. In Theatre.'

'He might have discussed it with me first!' Usually sour, Sister Chan became totally arctic. The telephone rang. 'Oh, yes, professor——' Kerrie tactfully left the room. Leon da Cruz could do his own explaining.

She showered and changed into plain narrow trousers and tunic in dark green lawn, made for her by Kim's Chinese tailoress. She had no intention of dressing up to visit Leon da Cruz, so she wore no make-up, and left her hair just falling naturally around her face. She had got over the helpless feeling he had aroused in her, and felt more confident and sure of herself. Just a short call, this evening, to be given a full list of her duties while they were away. Nothing to be apprehensive about. All the same, she didn't tell Kim where she was going.

The apartment, behind the main *klinik*, was a miniature palace. Soft lights, cream Chinese rugs and glowing wood set off the pale green chairs and comfortable-looking sofa. Dwarf palms were in every corner, silver and bronze Oriental statues and porcelain vases. And from some hidden speakers came the soft beauty of a Mozart piano concerto. Leon da Cruz was in casual trousers, and a short-sleeved shirt, open at the neck. Even like this he could have been the very Sultan Ali Tabatabai himself, as he stood, one leg relaxed, by the mahogany desk, leafing through a file.

'Come in, Kerrie,' he invited. His smile was natural. She could so easily forget at this moment that he was her chief, and a man she had vowed she could never like.

Once she was ensconced on that velvet sofa, with a glass of chilled white wine on an onyx side-table, he pulled a chair over to sit opposite to her, in informal comfort, while he explained what conditions she would meet the following day. In the opulence of her surroundings, Kerrie was glad that the meeting was perfectly businesslike. They spoke only of Kalang Bahru hospital, of the number of cases they would be dealing with, how long the operations would take, and how much time they had for planning and reorganising.

It was only when they had exhausted the agenda that he looked up with a smile and said, 'And that's that. Another glass of wine?'

'No, thank you.'

'I'll see you tomorrow, then. Be at the main door at eight.'

'Yes, sir.'

'I'm glad you're coming, Kerrie. I feel a lot happier about operating there now. It's been crying out for someone capable—like you—to begin to bring standards up.'

Kim caught up with her in the dining-room of their apartments. Over a plate of savoury *wanton mee*, Kerrie told her the news. 'Kalang? That's almost jungle. And why you?'

Kerrie shrugged. It wasn't her nature to boast that the professor wanted her for her talents. 'I suppose I'm the newest recruit, so I'm the one to be pushed around.'

'I'll miss you,' said Kim. 'Don't stay too long out there. And you'd better take your Malay phrase-book. The people out there might not speak English too well.'

Kerrie smiled at her friend. Kim had a square Malay face with pretty almond eyes, a tiny upturned nose and a generous mouth. 'I'll miss you like anything. You've been like a sister to me. And I don't mean a Sister Chan!'

'Tell you what—you can ring me,' said Kim. 'I'm on earlies next week, so I'll be here in the evenings.'

'I'll do that.'

'And tell me how you get on with da Cruz. You and he in the jungle sounds promising! A lot of girls would envy you this trip.'

Kerrie protested loudly, 'No way! I don't like him anyway. And don't forget that he has a beautiful fiancée. I'm sure the professor only wants an efficient theatre nurse.'

'Have you told Rick you're going?'

'He won't care.'

'He will, Kerrie. He told Jami what an asset you are to the *klinik*. He's making a pass at you, I can tell.'

Kerrie smiled. 'The feeling's mutual. He's a nice guy. But you know me, Kim—no involvements. Never trust a man, however nice. I'll be safe enough, don't you worry.'

'Even in the jungle?' grinned Kim.

'Especially in the jungle!'

CHAPTER THREE

KERRIE stood in the fresh green garden of the Sultan Ali Tabatabai Klinik in the sweet dew of early morning, and watched a heron feeding in the small pond between the nurses' home and the main hospital. The hazy sun diffused through the palm trees, already warm on her face. She was early, deliberately, because she wanted time to compose herself. It was difficult to believe that shortly, by the time the sun was at its most brilliant, she would be in the Malaysian jungle. She hadn't been at the *klinik* long, but already it was home, it was familiar—and Kalang Bahru was new and strange and, maybe, exciting.

She was gradually aware that she was not alone in the garden. Someone was standing in the shade of the veranda, watching her. She turned, shielding her eyes from the low rays of the sun. 'Good morning, Kerrie. You look like a wood goddess out there.' The delicate words sounded strange, coming from the mouth of the ultimate outdoor type in a broad Australian accent. But they sounded beautiful, all the same.

'Good morning, Rick.' She waited, as he came down the three steps and walked across the grass, sparkling with dew, towards her. He was wearing a black T-shirt and thin cotton trousers, and his feet were bare. She smiled at him. 'You're a most unconventional surgeon!'

'That's part of my charm, I guess.' He was looking at her, deep into her eyes, and his eyes were very blue in the luminous morning, as he bent and kissed her cheek lightly. 'I hear our chief is spiriting you away today.'

'I'm afraid so. But only for a couple of weeks.'

'Damn and blast the man.' Rick didn't raise his voice, and the words sounded odd, spoken in a normal conversational tone.

'I beg your pardon?'

'I said to hell with da Cruz and his rotten scheming mind!'

She looked up curiously 'What do you mean?'

'He's taking you because he knew we—you and I—were getting to know one another. He can't stand me being happy. He has to put his blasted spanner in the works whenever my happiness is concerned. It's sheer jealousy, Kerrie, I know it is. But that doesn't make it any more comfortable for me here.'

Kerrie stared. The tanned face was contorted with anger, though he still hadn't raised his voice, and the heron still grazed in the water. 'Are you sure? He showed me the plans of the hospital out there. It looks as though he's right—it does need a lot of work to get it running more smoothly.'

'Da Cruz is the only smoothie around here, Kerrie. God, one of these days he's going to get what's coming to him! When he falls, he'll fall hard, you'll see.'

A low voice from the entrance called across the garden. 'I didn't know you were in the habit of getting up early, Mr O'Grady.' Leon da Cruz moved forward, so that the light fell on his cool aristocratic face. 'Good morning, Kerrie. Is your bag in your flat?'

'No—I've put it in the foyer already.'

'Good. Then I'll have the car sent round. Are you ready?'

Kerrie looked up at Rick, who had folded his arms and was standing, his eyes fixed on the professor. 'Yes, I'm ready.' She said quietly, ''Bye, Rick. See you in a fortnight, I hope,' and began to walk towards the professor. But her arm was seized from behind, and Rick had folded her in a rough, uncomfortable embrace before she knew what was happening. He bent his head and kissed her lips, holding her head with both large hands so that she couldn't move. There was no tenderness in the kiss; it was stage-managed to give the maximum annoyance to Leon da Cruz. For a moment, Kerrie hated Rick for using her like that. He didn't have the right to kiss her—especially in that cavalier fashion. They were only friends. Even if he wanted to annoy the professor, he might have been more gentlemanly with her. Kim's warning echoed in her memory—only getting you to drop your guard. . . But then she remembered how much provocation Rick had received from Leon da Cruz, and she found it in her heart to understand him.

But as soon as he let her go she ran towards the hospital, panting with shock and discomfort. Leon da Cruz had not moved, but she could see that every muscle in his body was tensed, and his jaw jutted like a warrior's prepared for battle. The eyes were at their fiercest now, almost flashing thunderbolts at his unruly junior from under heavy black brows. Kerrie stood beside him, hoping that she never got on the wrong side of such dislike.

Rick stood for a full minute then, arms folded again, staring at them. Then he tossed his head in a gesture of dismissal and strode away across the gardens, until he was hidden by the cypress hedge.

Leon da Cruz unclenched his fists and blinked before turning to Kerrie. 'I hope he didn't hurt you. Shall we go?' And as he spoke his silver Pontiac slid almost silently from the shadows, driven by his chauffeur, who jumped out to open the door for them and to slide their luggage effortlessly into the boot.

Kerrie sat, saying nothing, still unnerved by the hatred she sensed in both men. They drove through the awakening town. Mopeds set off for work with their drivers, like a flock of buzzing bees. Housewives in bright sarongs washed steps and brushed pathways, and went off to market with large wicker baskets. The market itself was already bustling, filled with sacks of rice and chickpeas, squawking chickens tethered by one leg, freshly picked cabbages and ladies' fingers, mangoes, papaya, mangosteens and rambutans. Roadside cafés were opening for breakfast of rice cooked in coconut milk, slices of fried spiced meat, and savoury omelettes. Slowly the pageant before her soothed Kerrie's jangled feelings, and she sat back, calmer and resigned to the fact that somehow, without meaning to, she herself had aggravated the animosity between the two unwilling colleagues.

After the town, the road wound between grassy banks, and behind them either raw sprawling jungle or cultivated plantations of high rubber trees and squat palm oil trees in orderly rows. The professor had not spoken, but she knew he had been watching her. She felt strange at sitting next to him, on equal terms, when only days ago she had been an awe-struck newcomer, meeting her eminent employer for the first time. 'How do you like our countryside, Kerrie?'

'It's—very interesting.' She was still disturbed by his treatment of Rick. It just wasn't fair to treat your subordinates in that way.

'The east coast is on the other side of those plantations. It used to be only fishing villages, but the holiday tour operators have been prowling around. Big hotels are being built, and I'm afraid holiday villages in some parts. I suppose it's only progress, but I can't help regretting the passing of innocence for these people.'

'You sound as though you really care.'

He nodded. 'Why not? I was born in this state. True, I travelled. I studied in Australia for several years, and lectured in the States—my mother was half American. But I was right to come back. The country needs all its sons. We have a great future, if we have the right leaders.'

'You should go into politics yourself.'

'You think so, Kerrie?' He met her look. She hadn't looked at him before.

'If you care that much.'

He smiled suddenly. 'I'm afraid I don't stand fools gladly. You'll have noticed! That rules me out as a politician. No, I'll serve in the best way I can. Use my talents for my own countrymen as long as they want me.' They drove on for some miles, occasionally glimpsing the sea across fields of growing rice, with placid grazing water buffalo. He said quietly, 'And what about you? There must have been something in you that drew you to the mystical East?'

'Only that it was a good eight thousand miles from Brighton and Hove.'

'That's where you lived?'

'And worked, until my fiancé married someone else.'

There was a pause, then he said, 'I'm sorry. I know Brighton too—a pleasant town.'

She said ruefully, 'Please don't talk about it.'

'I understand entirely. We'll have coffee with a friend of mine I always call on when I drive this way. And then, as the hospital is only another few miles, we must get down to work.' As he spoke, a charming wooden house on stilts came into view round a bend, and the chauffeur turned into its little patch of garden. 'This is an old patient of mine, Kerrie. She would be most offended if I didn't call.'

They walked up the wooden steps together, and Kerrie noticed that he put his hand very gently on her waist. It was the touch of a butterfly, but it caused her heart to beat louder in her ears. Through the open door they could see a spry little woman in a brown batik sarong, polishing a brass ornament with vigour. The professor called, 'Moya? *Salaam*, Auntie.'

The little lady looked up, and her eyes twinkled with an elfin joy. '*Salaam*, my dear Leon, many *salaams*!' She ran towards him and took both his hands in hers. As the light from the door fell on her face, Kerrie realised that this lively lady was an old woman. Her brown face was lined, and the black hair in its tight bun on top of her head was streaked with silver.

'*Salaam*, Auntie,' he said again. He had to bend down quite a long way to kiss her cheek. His was a supple body, desirable. . . 'Back to Kalang again. How are you?'

'*Baiklah, baiklah, terimakasih*.' She stood back and saw Kerrie. '*Salaam* to your friend, Leon.'

He put his hand to Kerrie's back waist again, more firmly this time. It was an agreeable feeling, to sense his strength of body and mind like a great shield beside her. 'This is my colleague from England, Auntie. Kerrie is working at the Sultan, but has agreed to come and be my theatre assistant at the hospital for a while.'

Kerrie and the old lady bowed their heads to one another. Moya said, 'You are very welcome. You know Keri is a Malay word?'

'I didn't know. I hope it means something nice.'

Moya nodded. 'Oh, yes—very pretty.' She turned and shouted something in a piercing voice, and a young girl of about sixteen came out of a back room, and bowed shyly to the guests. 'Coffee, quick! Doctor, he is in a hurry.'

'No, we're not, Auntie—no operations today. We just want to look around and see what needs attention.'

Old Moya smiled at Kerrie, 'I was in that hospital one day—very bad smash-up. They all think I die.

But see—still here! Many thank yous to my dear Leon.'

Leon tried to stop her praises. 'It was you and your sheer guts, my dear. You enjoy life too much to give it up without a fight.'

The maid brought a brass tray with three cups and a tall pot of freshly made coffee. There was a little silver bowl containing sugar, but Moya made a great fuss when she saw that the milk was still in its supermarket carton. The girl was sent to put it in a jug, and came back with the milk in a pint measuring jug. Leon quickly poured the coffee, thanked the girl, and stopped further recriminations. 'This is always a pleasure.'

'It's lovely,' added Kerrie. 'So fresh.'

'Moya grows and roasts her own. See? Can you see the bushes in the back?' Leon pointed out of the window, which had no glass in it, just horizontal bars of wood, and a taut mosquito netting. Kerrie went over to look. As well as the coffee bushes, there were three rambutan trees, and under them a dun cow grazing, and three black goats.

She heard Moya whisper, 'English girl. American? Nice girl, Leon. You not let her get away.'

As Kerrie came back, Leon was smiling at Moya over his cup. He was saying, 'So that's your advice, Auntie?'

'Number one advice! You take, *lah*!'

Kerrie watched him, slightly embarrassed to have overheard a private conversation. Leon didn't answer, just gave what could have been a small nod—or it could have been a prelude to taking another sip of fragrant coffee.

They left soon afterwards, with a plastic bag full of ripe prickly red rambutans. 'You'll love these—refreshing,' said Leon. 'We'll have them after dinner tonight.' And the chauffeur started the car, putting away his own Thermos flask at the approach of his master. Kerrie thought how intimate it sounded, talking about having dinner together, as though they were close friends, instead of just a normal doctor-nurse partnership—a purely professional relationship.

They came across the Kalang Hospital in another twenty minutes. 'It's so pretty!' exclaimed Kerrie, forgetting that she wasn't really intending to speak too much to Leon. It stood, single-storeyed, among banks of dark green fruit trees and orange-flowered flame trees. It was a wooden building, painted pale blue, with white-shuttered windows and a sloping green tile roof.

'It could be.'

'What do you mean?'

'It's falling to pieces. That's why I haven't re-designed the operating theatre yet. I have an architect waiting to draw up plans for refurbishing, the moment we get the theatre customised. That's your job, Kerrie—and, if you can, to make the girls who work here treat it as a job, and not a part-time hobby. They're very laid-back here, can't wait to get out to the cinemas and the discos.'

'Young people are all like that.'

'Maybe, Kerrie—but the staff are disciplined in the Sultan. I want some of that discipline here.'

'You should have brought Sister Chan, then.'

Leon was striding ahead of her, eager to show her

the inside. At that comment he turned, stopping suddenly so that she bumped into him. Still holding her elbows to steady her, he said, 'You can't sentence me to that!'

She giggled, sharing the joke. And for a second or two he didn't let go, as they looked at each other like friends. No one would have been able to tell that Kerrie felt deeply uncomfortable having to be so close to a man she secretly felt she ought to despise. As the smile wore off, and he took his hands away, Kerrie answered quietly, 'She would have enjoyed it more than I.'

A shadow crossed his eyes, making them unreadable again. 'Well, better not make pre-judgements, Kerrie, when you don't know yet what you're going to see.' He rang at the large brass bell at the side of the high pale blue wooden doors, which were already ajar. Then he pushed the door and beckoned Kerrie to precede him into the building. As she brushed against his fresh white shirt, felt the heat from his body, he murmured, 'You know what pre-judging is, Kerrie? It's called prejudice.'

'I'm not prejudiced.'

'That's what I hoped.' He smiled, but his eyes were still shadowed. Then a smallish Malay man wearing nothing but a striped sarong came running along the corridor, calling '*Baiklah! Baiklah!*' When he saw Leon he grinned. 'Sorry, *tuan*—should have been at post. Went to eat some noodle, *lah.*'

'You are impossible, Han. Where's Matron?'

'She also eat the noodle, *tuan.*'

'And Dr Reza? Eating noodles?'

'No, *tuan*, Dr Reza doing the round of the ward.'

Leon sighed. 'So one person in the place is working, right?'

'*Baik*.'

Leon stroked his chin. 'Well, Han, this is Sister Snow, and she's come from the UK to sort things out around here. So you better let everyone know she's as fierce as a dragon.'

'Immediately, *tuan*.' But Han beamed at Kerrie, as if to let her know he didn't think she was a dragon at all, and would probably like to eat the noodle also.

Leon led the way to a dilapidated office on the right of the shadowy hallway. He sighed deeply. 'At least the lights are working. I hope the water supply is on.' He sat down at a large dark wood desk, and blew at the dust on it. 'Well, Kerrie? Want to give up now?'

'You can't run a hospital with no water supply!' Kerrie was appalled at the atmosphere of decay, of nobody caring.

'Oh, there is a supply. Han tends to turn it off at the mains to save it.' He put his head in his hands. His white shirt had gathered a coating of dust, and the dust from his hands was transferred to his forehead. Suddenly the big man, the consultant whom everyone feared and obeyed in Tajul, was weary, at a loss, and Kerrie felt a surge of pity towards him. He looked boyish, with the dust on his face, and from his attitude she realised what a large task faced them both, to bring this hospital up to the standard of the Sultan, against all the odds.

'You've put dust on your face.' She stood beside him to show him the marks, took his handkerchief from him to wipe them off. He face was turned up to her. She didn't know how it happened, but their faces moved closer together, and suddenly they were kissing each other. Leon rose to his feet, his mouth still holding hers, and his arms round her. She knew she ought to stop this, but her bodily longing was stronger than her will, and she clung to him, lost in the world of sensation and physical delight. The body that she had admired on the beach was unexpectedly and thrillingly moulded against hers, and it was too explosive a feeling for her ever to want it to end. His fingers meshed in her hair, and his lips left hers for a moment to move over her cheek, her neck, her throat, and back with increased passion to capture her lips again.

From a long way away, she heard footsteps on the wooden floor outside. Leon's arms loosed. In half a second he had regained the chair, while Kerrie slipped to the opposite side of the desk. She stood, holding on to the edge of the desk. When she looked up, she saw Leon's eyes were misty and sensual as they met hers. Her heart was wrung with physical loss, giving her a real stab of pain inside her chest. Where had all that pent-up emotion come from? Still breathing hard, she turned to see who was coming, hoping she retained a semblance of self-possession.

A slim young man in a white coat tapped on the half-open door before coming in. 'Leon, it's good to see you. How are you, old man?'

Leon stood to shake him by the hand, but sat down again quickly. 'Reza, how are things? Any further on with the designs?'

'Oh, yes, nearly done.'

'That's great. I've brought a friend from Tajul—Kerrie Snow. She's a terrific theatre sister. I thought she could help us—as an adviser as well as in Theatre.'

The doctor held his hand. 'Great stuff! Now we're getting somewhere. Nice to meet you, Kerrie. You don't mind first names?'

'Not a bit.'

Then mine's Yahiya.'

He was smiling too, so she said, 'Do I have to say that? Reza is easier.'

'Now I wonder why they all say that!' The atmosphere had returned to normal. It was clear Dr Reza was a nice man, running the hospital as well as he could, under the circumstances. 'My suggestion, Kerrie, is that you two get a shower—yes, Han has left the water on—and then come and have a good meal. The *mee* is good tonight.'

'So I gathered,' said Leon drily.

Reza turned back to Kerrie. 'And I'll show you the operating theatre tomorrow. I need to brush up the dead cockroaches first.'

Kerrie stared, not knowing how serious he was. 'I thought we were operating tomorrow.'

Reza laughed. 'I tend to exaggerate sometimes. You'll get used to me. But there are cockroaches. Kerrie, you must meet my wife. She's head of Physio here—well, actually, she's the only physio here. And with her qualifications she wouldn't be here at all except that for some reason she's crazy about me.' He waved cheerily and left them.

He left Leon and Kerrie still smiling. But, as they

faced each other, the smiles vanished. There was so obviously a sharp contrast between the easy, loving relationship of Reza and his wife, and the strained and highly charged emotional atmosphere that had startled both Kerrie and the professor with its intensity. He said, 'I'll show you where you'll be sleeping.'

'Thank you.'

'Shall we see if the bags have been brought in?' He walked to the door without looking at her. Kerrie didn't follow him. She was beginning to feel ashamed of her behaviour. To think that she had fallen so eagerly into his arms! Leon da Cruz, the creep who wouldn't let poor Rick build his own life in Tajul. The creep who was supposed to be engaged to a beautiful lady doctor. Belle Nader would have something to say about her beloved Leon's actions. How could he have done such a thing? How could Kerrie have allowed it? Leon came back. 'Are you coming?'

Quietly, with emphasis on every word, she said, 'Don't ever touch me again.'

He drew himself up. 'Don't worry—it was a mistake, nothing more. I apologise.' But he stifled another sigh, and, as she remembered the cockroaches, and looked around at the dilapidation around her, she understood something of what Leon must feel. There seemed to be no one in the place who cared as much as he did for improving their standards.

In spite of her determination, she said, 'There's a lot to do.'

He turned with a trace of relief in his eyes. 'Think we can make any impression?'

'We can try.' She walked past him into the hall. She knew he was watching her, as she followed the chauffeur and her bag towards her apartment. She could imagine the expression in those eyes, resigned, refined, aristocratic—and yet so very lonely.

Kerrie stepped warily into the room he indicated. It had a plain tiled floor, cool to the bare feet, as they had left their shoes at the front door in true Eastern custom. The floor was clean, but Reza's mention of cockroaches made Kerrie nervous, and she looked around carefully before stepping inside the room. Leon said, 'Don't worry, the room has been carefully prepared.'

'Prepared?'

'Sprayed with an insect repellent. There'll be no mosquitoes, and no other insects here. The windows are protected with mosquito netting, so if you keep your door closed you'll be quite all right.'

'Thank you. I'm sorry to be childish about these things.'

'It's understandable. You'll soon get used to them.' He pointed to a switch on the wall. 'I'm afraid there's no air-conditioning, so you'll need the fan.' He switched on, and a wooden ceiling fan began to rotate, making the oppressive air less uncomfortable. 'I'll leave you to get ready. There's a shower and toilet through that door. I'll come back for you in an hour.'

Kerrie sat on the double bed, with its simple cotton counterpane, and wondered why she had agreed to come. The hospital was primitive, the staff apparently lazy—and she had no one she could call a friend except her chief, to whom she was unwillingly but inevitably drawn. His sudden passionate embraces hadn't surprised her, feeling as she did an unexplained attraction as strong as Leon's. She put her head in her hands and wished Kim was here, to talk to and help her keep her head. As it was, she daredn't telephone, as she had promised. She could tell nobody about what had happened today between herself and Leon da Cruz.

CHAPTER FOUR

FORTUNATELY, life at Kalang Hospital proved nothing if not colourful. With the good-humoured Reza in charge, the staff were happy, if rather lackadaisical, and the patients got better with a smile. But the reverse of this was that many of the staff were lazy, and the good-humoured Reza never reprimanded anyone. Kerrie, however, forgave him this, so relieved was she to have this happy man giving the entire hospital an atmosphere of cheerfulness, which was a splendid antidote to Leon's brooding intensity.

They operated for most of the next morning. Leon was totally detached and correct. Kerrie, apprehensive at first about meeting him after that unexpected show of affection, began to relax. She tied his mask and gown behind him, and then held his gloves for him to slide his fingers into. Their eyes met. He murmured so that no one else could hear, 'You sure you're all right? You have forgiven me for yesterday? You'll work with me as if you were still in the Sultan?'

'Of course.' His humility disarmed her. 'It's my job.'

'Good. Thank you, Kerrie. As you see, I'm going to need all the help you can give me, operating single-handed, without an assistant surgeon.'

He withdrew his second gloved hand from hers.

She felt a sense of loss at losing contact with him, and was annoyed with herself for feeling it. 'I'm ready,' she told him.

Standing at his side, engrossed in the mechanics of a serious double hernia repair, Kerrie forgot she was annoyed with him, and began to feel a professional as well as a personal sense of fulfilment, to be working with such an expert craftsman. The cases were wheeled in rapidly, so fast did those skilled hands work, and so well did surgeon and sister work together, so that by lunchtime eight patients were either in the recovery annexe or had already been returned to their wards.

'Lunch in the garden, I think.' Leon stripped his theatre gear, and it was immediately whipped away by the maid.

'She isn't one of the lazy ones,' Kerrie pointed out.

'They're always on their best behaviour when I'm here. It's how to make them realise that standards have to be maintained—not just to please me, but because a mistake in a hospital could be fatal. One wrong medication, one misdiagnosis. It's a nightmare I live with—ever since I bought the place.'

'Why did you buy it in such a state?'

He seemed embarrassed at the question. 'The State government were going to close it down.' He bent to slip on his sandals. 'See you in the garden. You're looking tired.'

Kerrie stood for a moment. So Leon had put his own money in a hospital in a poor area, simply to provide a service for the local people. He couldn't possibly make money out of it. Everything she had

learned about Leon da Cruz here was good—the
patients he had cured adored him, Reza and the
staff admired him greatly, and she could see for
herself what would happen to these surgical cases if
he weren't here. They would either suffer in silence,
or die. There was very little chance that they could
afford to get to a big town for an operation. Kerrie
walked along the corridor to the overgrown, luxur-
iant back gardens, thinking hard.

'This is Bob, our architect, Kerrie.' At a buffet
table covered with curries and salads and chapatis,
Leon was chatting to a thin stooped man with a mop
of reddish hair and a sheaf of papers he didn't know
what to do with as he juggled his plate and a fork.
'You can take a look at the plans after lunch.'

A gust of wind blew the plans all over the grass.
Laughing, Reza suggested they wait until later to
look at them. 'After all, we have such a good cook
here, it's a pity to mix business with eating.'

Leon said with a smile, 'I'm quite aware that
eating is the national pastime around here, Reza.
Sometimes I think people get appendicitis on purpose, just to stay here for a few days!'

Kerrie was asked what she thought of the theatre.
'I've never worked in a theatre with bare wooden
boards. I can believe you about the cockroaches,
Reza. Would it be sensible to put a plastic floor
covering down? If the joints are sealed, I'd feel a lot
more hygienic.'

Bob made a note. 'How about the size? You all
comfortable with the size?'

'It could be smaller, if you think we could make
three rooms out of these two, and buy a third

operating table.' The talk became technical, and Kerrie's mind wandered. Then she remembered she ought to telephone Kim. Excusing herself, she made her way to the single phone, in Leon's room. The room had been thoroughly cleaned, and smelt fresh today. There was even a white orchid in a jar on the desk. Kerrie dialled the nurses' home. Kim should be back from her early shift.

'Hello?' A man's voice. A visitor, perhaps.

'Could I speak to Kim Mayang, please, if she's there?'

'That's Kerrie, isn't it?'

The accent was unmistakable then. 'Rick! What are you doing there?'

'Never mind that, love. How are you? How are you bearing up under the strain of working for Mr Big? I'm missing you.'

'All right, thanks.' Her voice sounded tense. She hoped Rick didn't read more into it. She didn't want anyone ever to know about that passionate episode between the professor and herself. 'There are two more operating days, and then two more to make sure the patients are doing all right. There's the architect's meeting. After that, we have planning meetings, and a surveyor's coming to check everything with the architect. With luck, I'll be back in Tajul by the following weekend, by myself. Le—the prof is going on to Kuala Lumpur.'

'I'll be waiting, sweetheart. You don't know how it stuck in my throat, seeing you driving off in that bastard's car. He isn't your type, Kerrie—you must see that by now. I'm well aware that women find him attractive, and I only hope you're keeping him at arm's length.'

'I agree with you—not my type. It's only a business trip, you know.'

'For you, maybe. But that man would do anything to get at me. Even make a pass at you.'

Kerrie felt her fingers tighten round the phone. 'Don't worry, I'm not interested—and he's supposed to be engaged, isn't he? I'm sure we'll survive for two weeks.'

'Ring me the minute you get back. Please, love?'

'All right, Rick. Is Kim there?'

'No. I came to see her—to ask her for news of you, but there's no one in her flat.'

'So will you tell her I called?'

'Sure thing. Cheers, Kerrie. See you soon.'

As she put the phone down slowly, Kerrie gave a little start. Leon was standing at the door, watching her. How much had he heard? His voice was cool. 'Missing him, were you?'

Kerrie stood up, and stood her ground. 'I think what I do in my own time is counted as private, don't you?'

'You're not a child, Kerrie. I know you're entitled to live your own life, but you don't know this man you're defending, that's all.'

'I'll be charitable, and take it you're telling me this for my own good. Well, thank you. There's no need to mention it again.'

'Very well, I won't.'

Even when they were arguing, angry with one another, she felt his magnetism like a physical force. It wasn't just the dominating eyes, the regal tilt of the head, the sculpted perfection of his features. She felt as she had when she first saw him, a great need to touch, hold and possess him. She had to speak, to keep him near, just for a little while, even though she despised herself for doing it. 'You aren't phoning your fiancée?'

'If you mean Dr Nader, she is not my fiancée. She's also a busy woman, and I wouldn't dream of disturbing her by telephoning during the day.' He leaned against the door-frame. The atmosphere was intensely warm, and she could see beads of sweat on his face. He lifted an eyebrow slightly and said with a trace of sarcasm, 'I wonder what Mr O'Grady is doing, to be able to come to the telephone. He ought to be holding a minor surgical clinic at two.' The dark eyes never moved from her face. Then he stood up straight, as if wanted to end the wrangling, and his tone was considerate. 'Come along, Kerrie. You look exhausted in this heat—I think you could do with a short siesta. You aren't used to working without air-conditioning.'

He was right. Sweat was forming on her forehead too, and the back of her neck, dampening her hair into streaks. 'I think I will, if you don't need me,' she agreed.

'Turn the fan up high. Don't want you coming down with fever.'

'I had all the injections.'

'That's good. Try and rest; I'll send someone to wake you at three.' His soft voice sounded caring. It was no wonder his patients felt better after he visited them at their bedsides. There was more to good surgery than just a good pair of hands. He came into the room, pulled the chair out ready to sit down. Kerrie slipped past him, trying not to touch, after what had happened last time. But he caught her elbow and turned her to face him for a second, and there was a strange sad look on his face as he let her go.

They operated the following morning, again a long list. They spoke little in the heat, only saying what was necessary. Kerrie found herself remembering that first kiss, and wondering if he had thought about it as she had, maybe wondered what electricity had drawn them so closely together. In the afternoon they all rested, and then Kerrie, Leon, Reza and Bob sat down in the cool of the evening in the garden and discussed the progress of the repairs.

By that time Kerrie had a good idea of the content of the theatre cupboards, and wrote out a list of equipment they would need as soon as the basic structure was sound, and the new flooring put down. Leon said, 'If we're lucky, that could be in place for our next visit, Kerrie.'

So he wanted her to come with him again. She didn't mind. She was becoming fond of the little hospital, with its bright jays and wood pigeons in the overgrown gardens. Reza and his pretty wife Polly were good company, and Kerrie felt somehow glad that she was helping the poorer members of society, not just the wealthy who could afford the luxurious care they received at the Sultan.

She didn't telephone again. Rick would tell Kim when she would be back. She tried not to think of Rick O'Grady, and of the bitterness that sparked when the two men met. It would be better at the

Sultan when Leon was absent—yet without Leon da Cruz she knew the Sultan would seem to be without its heart.

On the last day of the assignment, after an exhausting session of last-minute minor operations, and a ward round to see all the others, Kerrie lay on her bed, thinking about the way Leon had looked at her, as he thanked her. 'You've been my right hand, Kerrie, you know that?' She recalled that look, and the effect it had on her, while the fan at full blast cooled the air a little, but made such a noise that she thought she wouldn't sleep. She felt hot, yet she shivered, and for a moment pulled the thin coverlet over her, until sweating made her push it away again.

It seemed to be many hours later. The fan still rotated, but it was dark outside and she could hear the night crickets chirping their shrill chorus. Was dinner over? She tried to get up, but felt weary and desperately weak. She was agonisingly thirsty, but found she didn't have the energy to pull herself off the bed to get to the kitchen for a drink of iced water from the big fridge. Worried now, she called out, 'Please, is anyone there? Could you help me?' And her voice sounded pathetically far away.

She must be ill. Malaria! Surely not—she had taken the drugs prescribed. She mustn't panic. But she felt pains in her chest when she breathed in, and closed her eyes in fear. Tears slipped from under her eyelashes.

Then, miraculously, after what felt like hours, she felt a cool hand on her brow, and her face was gently wiped with a damp cloth. She knew from the smell

of crisp cotton shirt and aftershave that it was Leon.
'I'm sorry——'

'Sh—no need to talk. You're OK. Would you like
a drink of water?'

Her lips felt dry and cracked. 'Oh, yes, please.'
He put his arm gently round her to help her up on
the pillows. Her head ached badly, but the drink
was like ambrosia to her parched throat. 'What's the
matter with me?'

Leon didn't take his hand away. She didn't want
him to. It was comforting and safe, and Kerrie knew
what good hands she was in. Her head was leaning
against his shoulder, and if she had been stronger
she would have enjoyed the experience. 'It must be
a form of fever, Kerrie. Have you any mosquito
bites?'

'Yes, a few—small ones. That night, when we had
the meeting outdoors.'

'Most of the mosquito strains are harmless in this
area. It's my fault, bringing you here when you're so
new to Malaysia. That's something I should have
thought about, but we haven't had any trouble for
so long—and the strains, as I said, don't usually
carry anything nasty. I was selfish—thinking only of
my own work, of how you were the best person for
the job.' He sounded upset, blaming himself so
openly.

Kerrie wanted to soothe him, stop him being
angry with himself. 'No, don't say that.' Her voice
was little more than a croak, and her throat ached.

He looked down at her, and held her closer
against him while he wiped her face again and
smoothed back her hair. She felt his breath cool on

her hot cheeks. 'I'll get Reza's wife to undress you and make you comfortable.'

'I'll be all right soon.'

'No, Kerrie—I'm afraid you're going to be uncomfortable for a few days. I can't have you getting up.'

Beginning to get frightened, she whispered, 'What is it? Dengue?' The fever everyone dreaded, because there was no cure.

Leon took out his stethoscope. 'Let me listen to your chest.' She felt no embarrassment as he examined her carefully with capable hands, sounded her chest and checked her eyes and her reflexes. 'Yes, I'm afraid so. You know there isn't any treatment, Kerrie—you must be patient, and wait for your own body to make antibodies to the virus. It could be two weeks.' He laid her gently back on the bed. 'We'll look after you. You mustn't worry.'

She felt too weary to worry too much—and a bit scared too. But she remembered his problems through her own pain. 'You'll have no help in Theatre.'

'Don't worry about that. I'll have a nurse sent out.'

'Could I have more water, please?' Her voice was hoarse, and she felt guilty, being nursed by a consultant. But there was no one else to ask, and she felt miserably ill. The room seemed to spin round at times, and she felt stifled, wrapped in cotton wool, unable to get out.

Leon held her again while she drank. Before letting her sink back against the pillow, he bent his head and kissed her hot forehead. His voice was little more than a blur, as he whispered, 'Poor little thing! I'm so sorry, my dear.'

The next set of cool hands she felt belonged to Reza's wife, Polly. In the next two weeks she was washed down, her nightclothes changed, and she was encouraged to drink as much as she could. One morning she heard men's voices, and the sound of wood being sawed and nails being hammered. The next time she looked up, a new fan had been installed in the ceiling, a large fan with four swishing blades, so much quieter than the small old creaking one.

Polly came in next morning. Kerrie was unsure of the date, or the time. But for the first time her vision was clear, and she could see what a pretty, lively girl she was, so cheerful that it raised Kerrie's spirits to see her smile. 'You've been very kind to me,' Kerrie said.

Polly smiled. 'You must be getting better—you haven't wanted to talk for over two weeks! I'm so glad, Kerrie. We've been awfully worried. Leon sat up all night when the delirium was at its worst.'

Leon—watching over her. So close she felt to him, and so grateful. Maybe that was why she was recovering so well. She wished she had seen his kind face as he watched over her. 'I feel more human— but so weak. What a useless theatre sister I turned out to be.' Over two weeks she had been like this, As Leon had predicted. 'Is Professor da Cruz——?'

'He cancelled his visit to Kuala Lumpur Klinik and the University. He stayed here to look after you,' Polly told her.

'But—the operations—he had people waiting in KL.'

'He got a colleague from the National Hospital to stand in for him.'

After Polly had gone, Kerrie tried to pull herself up and look around. But she fell back, exhausted. Leon had put off everything to stay with her. It was a kindness she didn't deserve. She had never wanted to be in a position of gratitude to him. She wondered what Rick was doing, and if he knew she had been ill. He couldn't have come to see her—not with Leon being in charge. The two men clearly kept as far away from one another as possible.

The maid came in with a tray. 'Polly she say you over the worst, Kerrie, so I bring you nice pot of tea.'

Kerrie suddenly felt ravenous. 'That's wonderful! I never thought I'd miss a simple cup of tea. I feel as though I haven't had one for years. Thank you—*terimakasih*.'

Then she heard Leon's voice, as the maid pulled a bed-tray up where Kerrie could reach it. 'Do you mind if I pour? I think you'll find your hands still very weak.'

She looked up at him, aware what a waif she must look, with her tangled hair spread over the pillow, and her face paler as her tan had worn off a little indoors. But Leon's expression was one of gentle relief. She knew she had to be honest with him now. No false modesty, and no childish standoffishness now. Not after what he had done for her. She said, 'I can't find the right words to thank you.'

'Then let me see you enjoy your tea. How about

a little slice of buttered toast?' He poured two cups. She watched his face, and for a moment couldn't even think of the bad side of his character. Today she knew he had saved her life, and she had no way of showing her gratitude to him. He bent over her and lifted her up against the pillows as though she weighed nothing at all. His arms were strong and warm against her body.

'Am I well enough to go back to Tajul?'

'Yes, I'm afraid so.'

'You don't sound sure. Why afraid?'

He shook his head slowly. 'For the simple reason that I won't be there to keep an eye on that Australian ape—I have to go to KL. I know I promised not to mention it again, Kerrie, but it matters to me. You will be careful? Don't believe every word he says?'

'Leon, is there nothing about him that you like? I mean, why is he working for you when you seem so opposed to each other? Why does he stay?'

Leon held both her hands for a moment and looked into her eyes. 'Drink your tea.' He supported her while she picked up her cup and sipped fragrant tea. 'Good, isn't it?'

'It's blissful, Leon—but why won't you answer my questions?'

'Because you mustn't talk too much on your first day of recovery.'

'I can listen.'

He smiled at that, and leaned over to stroke her cheek. 'But you mustn't. Doctor's orders, dear. You should sleep now. I'll organise transport back to Tajul tomorrow—if you're good.'

Kerrie remembered smiling her thanks to him as he left the room. It had sounded so natural when he called her 'dear'. It was becoming very easy to ignore his unreasonable treatment of Rick, and the veiled animosity between the two men, so marked that morning when she'd left Tajul with Leon. Kerrie slept then, still wishing for an explanation. This time it was a calm, natural sleep.

The luxury ambulance that came from KL to take her back to Tajul was padded with cushions, foam-filled and five-star. As Kerrie and her belongings were arranged inside, she began to fear she wouldn't be able to thank everyone who had looked after her. Where was Leon? Reza and Polly came to say goodbye. It was as they were leaving that the driver began to shut the doors. So Leon wasn't going to see her off.

How could she be disappointed? True, she had felt a deep attraction to him, and a longing for his company. But that was only because he was a handsome and very kind man, and a good surgeon. They had been close lately, but perhaps it was only because he had been looking after her so tenderly. Perhaps it meant nothing more to him than a kindly bedside manner.

She had to remember he was still a man who treated his junior as an inferior, a proud man, overly aristocratic and scornful where Rick O'Grady was concerned. She should be glad she wasn't seeing him this morning. She mustn't let her natural gratitude hide his true character.

The doors opened again, and she felt a shiver of hope. But it was a woman who climbed in and sat down in the seat beside Kerrie's stretcher. Her voice was beautiful, soft and caring. 'Hello, Kerrie—I'm Belle Nader. I'm on my way back from KL and Leon asked me to travel with you. I'm going back to Tajul too, so I can keep a friendly eye on you. Are you quite comfortable?'

Dr Belle Nader. Kerrie turned her head to look at the exquisitely dressed woman, with her pile of glossy hair, her slim figure, her tailored grey silk suit—and on her left hand a huge, glittering solitaire diamond. 'Thank you, yes,' she said.

Leon had said he wasn't engaged, but this looked very much like an engagement ring to Kerrie. Anyway, Belle lived up to her name. She was physically as beautiful as Leon was—an excellent match. He would be crazy not to marry her. Belle said, 'You came out with Leon, I believe. Why on earth did he take a newcomer? Everyone knows it's safer to stay in the towns until you get acclimatised.' She looked more closely at Kerrie, who was feeling better, though weak, and had taken the trouble to comb her hair and look a little bit more human. 'Hmm, you're very pretty. Maybe that's the reason.'

Kerrie protested, 'You don't really think that Professor da Cruz would take a nurse with him just because she had a nice face? To Kalang? You can't operate without an experienced theatre sister—not in that place. You know Leon wouldn't do a thing like that. He cares too much about the quality of his work.'

'Believe me, young lady, you can in the jungle. You can operate single-handed if you have to. Leon has done it, more than once. No, that's just the tale he's been spinning to you, Kerrie, believe me, to get you along. But don't worry, it's nothing to do with me whom he chooses to take with him.'

'But, Dr Nader——'

'Call me Belle, dear. Everyone does.'

'Belle, the professor doesn't seem that sort of person. He's always very proper. I don't think he'd lie. Especially. . .' Kerrie took a deep breath, but dared to go on with what she was thinking, 'Especially when I understand he's. . .well, you and he—and I have a boyfriend, too.' The words came out with a rush.

Belle looked at her ring, and made the lovely stone flash with blue lights as she twisted it on the delicate honey-coloured finger. 'So you know about us?'

'I—was told.'

The other woman fixed Kerrie with her pretty eyes. 'I suppose you've been told the story of his princess? It makes a nice fairy-story, doesn't it? In western fairy tales the princess always marries the woodcutter. In the East we are a little bit more practical, about these things. Princesses marry royalty, or they don't marry at all.'

'I think that's sad. I think a professor is good enough for a princess—if they're in love.'

'Love is a very overrated word, Kerrie. Devalued in the West into sexual frenzy.'

And Kerrie felt herself blushing. That kiss she had shared with Leon—was that mere sexual frenzy? It had seemed inevitable at the time—completely overwhelming. But she still wanted to argue. Belle Nader seemed quite prejudiced against the West. Or was it

Kerrie herself she disliked? 'Have you been to the West? There are as many decent couples with the same values——'

Belle didn't appear to like being told what to think. 'Kerrie, try to sleep. It's a long journey, not very smooth when we get to the poorer roads, and you're still very far from being a healthy girl.'

'Yes, Belle.' Kerrie was tired. A pause, as they jolted along, with only the engine noise for company. Then Kerrie said sleepily, 'Do you think you'll marry soon?'

'I? I doubt it.' Belle twisted the ring again, and her pretty face was contorted with some deep emotion for a second. Kerrie turned away, pretending she hadn't noticed.

CHAPTER FIVE

KERRIE was assigned one of the luxury rooms in the nursing wing of the Sultan Ali Tabatabai Klinik. She had only been made comfortable there for a few minutes by two of the juniors when Sister Chan came bustling in. 'Well, Kerrie, that wasn't a very successful trip.'

'No, Sister.' She was surprised to be called by her first name. Maybe, as a patient, she became entitled to more of Sister Chan's goodwill? 'It turned out that I wasn't much help at all in the end.'

Sister actually smiled. 'The professor won't take new girls again, I'm sure. I don't know why I wasn't asked before you.'

'Probably because you're so invaluable here, Sister.'

Sister's look showed that she mistrusted Kerrie's attempt at a compliment. 'Maybe. Now, as you're a normally healthy young woman, I expect you to be up and about quite soon. There are no restrictions on your getting up. Tiredness will stop you doing it too often at first. But you're not to leave the room without permission, is that clear?'

'Yes, Sister.'

'And no visitors without my permission. If any of your friends pop in, send them to me to make sure it's all right.'

After Sister had bossed her as much as she could,

and could think of no more rules and regulations to expound, Kerrie was left alone. The bed was supremely comfortable, the air neither cold nor hot, the room scented with flowers. Kerrie slept, only marginally wondering about Leon da Cruz, and when she would see him again. Belle Nader had not denied their affair, yet she hadn't wanted to talk about it. Kerrie was curious, but she was also weary.

She spent much of the next three days sleeping. Sometimes she dreamed of a mysterious sultan in gold turban and robes who lived in the Kalang Hospital, and rocked her in his arms. The rest did her good, and the good food soon gave her strength. She realised Kim had not been given permission to visit. But she wasn't really ready for visitors. On the fourth day, she began to feel restless. She walked unsteadily around the bed a few times, then lay on it, dressed in her flowered cotton housecoat.

The door opened. She expected only Sister, but the healthy-looking blue-eyed figure filling the door-way was Rick O'Grady's. Her heart swelled. Life was beginning to get back to normal. 'Oh, Rick, how nice to see you!' she exclaimed.

He was still in his theatre gown. 'Honey, I only heard today you were home. Why didn't you call me?' He was at her side in two strides, holding her face in his hands, kissing her. 'Sweetheart, I was so worried! They said it was bad. They said at one stage it was touch and go.' He pulled her into his embrace. 'Poor kid! Poor Kerrie. Anyway, you're back now, and I'm going to look after you.'

'Thanks—but please don't crush my ribs, Rick.'

'I missed your sweet face, Kerrie. The place

wasn't the same without you.' He kissed her again, more gently this time. He hadn't kissed her like that before. 'We're going to have a ball when you're out of here—I'll make up for all the miserable days and nights you had out there. That bastard should never have taken you. He only did it to show me he has more power than I do—to keep me in my place—in his shadow!'

Kerrie didn't answer. Rick was warning her against Leon, who was warning her against Rick. The two men could act like children if they wanted to. But what was bothering Kerrie at that moment, in between Rick's kisses, was that she didn't like being kissed by him. She had agreed to go out with Rick because it was a light-hearted friendship. The way he was mauling her now was definitely not light-hearted—and she wanted him to stop.

'What can I get you, love? Flowers? Candy? Perfume? You name it and it's yours.'

'Ask me in a day or two. I'm too sleepy to think just yet.' She wasn't sleepy at all, but suddenly she wanted him to stop pawing her as though she somehow belonged to him. He left her after another few minutes, and Kerrie lay back, wishing he hadn't shown so much attention towards her. Kim's warning about the number of nurses he had dated rang in her mind. His technique was certainly very clever; it sounded genuine. But Kerrie couldn't help remembering Leon's kiss. Now that was a real kiss, something she would never forget, something that even thinking about made her feel warm and languorous.

Next morning she was awake early, knowing that she was cured. She felt fit, hungry, and eager to get out of this little room and back to work. There was a knock on the door. 'Come in,' she called. She was sitting on the edge of the bed, in her housecoat, deciding to take a shower and get dressed in day clothes for the first time.

The figure who crept on silent feet into the room made her cry out with joy. 'Oh, Madame Karela! You're well!'

'Yes, my dear—and you are not. Is there anything I can do for you?'

'You've already done it by getting better!' Kerrie patted the bed. 'Sit by me. It's so incredible to see you walking about—I'm so happy for you. Maybe we can have breakfast together.'

'That is what I asked Sister. I shall be going home in a day or two. I am very grateful to you for the way you showed me such patience and gave me strength to go on fighting.'

Kerrie said, '*Madame*, I only did my job.'

'So, my kind little nurse, tell me what has happened to you—apart from this dreadful fever?'

'Well. . .' Kerrie smiled, realising the little lady's appetite for gossip. 'What would you say if I told you I've got man problems?'

'That is good! Last time we talked your heart was broken.'

Kerrie laughed. 'So it was. Well, this isn't as straightforward as it might be. I hope it doesn't sound too complicated! The man I think I love is engaged to someone else. Also there are certain things about him I don't like. He doesn't know my feelings, by the way. I've only worked them out since being cooped up in bed, because I can't get him out of my mind.'

'I know just what you mean. Go on.' Madame Karela patted her hand. 'We women, we love to think we know all the answers!'

The nurses came in then, with breakfast for two. They laid a small table, and the two ladies in their robes, one patient silver-haired and one golden, sat opposite one another and shared Kerrie's secret. Kerrie poured the coffee, and they ate fresh rolls with butter and marmalade, and sliced sweet oranges and papaya. Kerrie went on with her story, delighted to be able to get it off her mind to someone who wouldn't know who the man was. Madame Karela would be far away in a day or two; she was going to her son in Singapore to recuperate. 'Now there is someone who likes me, and whom I like but don't love, I think he's a nicer person than the other.'

'I see.'

'My question is, shall I remain faithful to my ideal man, whom I love but don't like, even though he shows no signs—well, hardly any—of feeling the same way about me, and is engaged? Or shall I live a normal life, go around with the other, nicer, man, and try to forget my true love?' Kerrie smiled, pleased to see the look of bewilderment on her new friend's face.

Madame Karela smiled too, delighted to be confided in, as she cut herself another slice of papaya and speared it daintily with a silver fork. 'You are making light of this, my dear. But I shall answer seriously—just in case I can really help. You must live a normal life, of course. But there is just one thing. You said your ideal man had shown some signs of caring. How strong were those signs?'

Kerrie remembered the feeling of Leon's arms going round her, both he and she unable to hold back from that hungry embrace. 'Beautiful,' she whispered, almost to herself.

Madame said quietly, 'Then perhaps you should ask yourself what it is you don't like about him, and try to see why.'

'He's unjust—not to me, but to someone else.'

Madame smiled. 'Then, Kerrie, I think you know the answer.'

'Yes—yes, I do. I have to forget about him, don't I?

'Of course. Injustice is something that can't really be forgiven.'

'You're right. When I say the word out loud, it makes him ugly—however handsome he really is.'

'It sounds very much like it.' But *madame*'s dark eyes were thoughtful, as she took her leave. 'Kerrie, I know you intended this as a bit of fun. If you are really unhappy—any time in the future, I mean— I'd like to think I could help. You've had enough sadness already over a man. My advice is to stay away from them all for a while.'

'That's exactly what I mean to do!'

Rick came round to the nurses' home that evening, after Kerrie had walked slowly across the garden while Kim carried her things. Kim saw him coming. 'Rick, you've come at the right time—we're welcoming Kerrie home. You can join us if you like.' Kim indicated the feast of noodles, chicken, fried prawns, spiced omelette and cashew rice the kitchen staff had laid out in the dining-room.

Rick grinned his crooked, attractive grin, 'Hi.' He bent to kiss Kerrie's cheek. 'I came to take you to dinner.'

'Oh, Rick, we've got dinner here—I couldn't come, not now. Stay?'

'No—no, thanks.' He was quick to refuse the invitation, protesting that he would be in the way. 'Meet me later, then?'

'Where?'

'I'll be waiting.'

The eyes of the other girls watched Kerrie as she came back. To their credit, no one said anything. But she knew what they were thinking; poor Kerrie—latest in the line of Rick's conquests. She sat down, and pretended nothing was wrong. Now was the time to live up to her decision not to allow herself to become serious about any man. It was the only way.

It was more than two hours before she remembered his words. 'I'll be waiting.' Against her better judgement, as the party began to split up, she slipped out into the velvety night. Rick was there, standing alone in the shadows. She felt sorry for him—badly done to by Leon, when all he wanted to do was build a life for himself.

'Thanks for coming, sweetheart. Shall we go along to the club for a quiet drink?' He sounded subdued.

'Sure.' As they walked to the Sultan Klinik's own social club, Kerrie felt safe with him. No more kissing, then, if they were to sit openly in the club. 'Anything wrong, Rick? You're quiet.'

'Nothing wrong. Wait till you hear!' And once they had found a quiet table in an alcove, near enough to be able to hear the pianist playing smoochy music, Rick said in a low voice, 'I've found a place of my own, honey. I wanted you to be the first to know!'

'That's wonderful! Where?'

'About three miles away—other side of town.'

'Leon can't possibly object to that.'

Rick looked up from his beer quite sharply. 'First-name terms with the chief?'

Blushing, Kerrie said, 'In Kalang everybody used first names. It's an informal place.'

'And what did you get up to informally with him?'

'Nothing!'

He was watching her now, wary. 'You won't go running to him with this news?'

'Don't be silly, Rick. I'm on your side—I think he's treated you abominably. I wish you luck.'

'How would you like to work for me when I get started up? Top job—Nursing Administrator?'

'So that's what you wanted me for!' Kerrie laughed.

'Sure. One of the things.' He grinned again. 'What do you say, love? Tempting prospect?'

Kerrie didn't answer at once. She had only just got back to the Sultan, and to her friends. Moving away was the last thing she wanted. But she tried to show an interest. 'When will you be operational?'

'About two months, I think. Decorate and furnish the place—nice bit of brass plate with my name on it. Say you'll come?'

'Can I think it over?'

He seemed irritated by her failure to seize his offer. But he said grudgingly, 'Of course you can. It's a big career decision. Don't forget, love, that, with da Cruz, you'll never get further than Sister. With me, you could be one of Tajul's leading citizens. A share of the profits, the lot. You think it over, sweetheart. I'd be getting the best—and so would you.'

Kerrie held her hand out and took his. 'Congratulations, anyway. I wish you all the luck in the world.'

'Thanks. When the groundwork's done, I'll show you round.'

'Any staff accommodation?'

'There'd be room in my place—there are three bedrooms in the flat above the *klinik*.'

She smiled. 'You're not serious? I wouldn't do that!'

Rick made it appear as though he hadn't said what he said. 'Don't worry—lots of places for rent. Belle might have room at her pad.'

'Belle?'

He looked slightly uncomfortable then. 'Well, she's been—advising me a little. She thinks I'm doing the right thing. As soon as I get the staff situation sorted, we'll find a staff block somewhere. Anyway, not to worry. Now that I've found the ideal site, the other things will happen, I'm sure of it.'

'So am I.' She was happy for him. Leon's unaccountable jealousy had proved ineffective. 'What are you going to call it?'

He smiled broadly. 'What do you think? There's

only one thing bigger than a sultan—and that's a maharajah!'

'The Maharajah Klinik? Hmm, not bad. It rolls off the tongue, Rick.'

'Let's hope it rolls in the money, love!'

He left her at the door of the nurses' home, with a kiss that was undemanding and warm. She liked that. If he could remain undemanding, Rick would make a good friend, and she had to admit she liked the sound of his new place, and wished him well in it. She wandered in the garden, drinking in the smell of the jasmine and the frangipani that lay on the night air like honey. Was she tempted to be a nursing administrator—it sounded good? Top job, top money. After all, she didn't owe Leon anything. He could always replace her—his hospital was a prestige one. All the same, it would be a wrench, because she had been so happy here. The Sultan was the first place to take her in its arms after her broken heart. And anyway, could she legally take her work permit with her? Surely it wouldn't be allowed so easily.

There was a sudden sound of voices. A shout— 'Help, doctor, a doctor, please, in Allah's name!' And a group of men came round the corner, carrying another in their arms. Kerrie's training was absolute. She jumped up and went towards the voices.

Rick O'Grady hadn't been far away. He went towards them too, and she heard his voice clearly. 'What do you want? This is a private *klinik*, we can't take casualties. Get him to the Government hospital quickly.'

'He got money, *tuan* doctor. Help, for Allah's sake, please help!'

Rick went and pulled the cloth back from the man's face. It was covered in blood. 'Doesn't look like he's got a bean. He's probably finished anyway.' He felt the pulse briefly, and said, 'Take him away.'

Kerrie stared at him in amazement and horror. 'No!' she shouted in anguish. 'No, Rick, you can't!'

'No, let's take a look at him.' A quiet voice, a gentle commanding voice that Kerrie recognised immediately. Leon had also heard the frightened voices. He bent over the prostrate form. 'He's bleeding—it could be fatal. We'll try and stop it. Bring him in, please.'

Kerrie ran down the sloping embankment. 'Let me give you a hand,' she called. Rick's attitude had been callous beyond belief. She ran alongside the men as they carried the patient into an examination-room. She found a cloth and gently wiped the blood from the man's face and neck, so that Leon could examine him and find out the source of the bleeding. She waved the patient's friends out of the room.

Rick followed them in. 'Need a hand, Chief?'

Leon looked up briefly. 'No, thank you. You're better out of here, O'Grady.'

Kerrie understood Leon's feelings of disgust. But, though Rick had acted badly, he was offering to help now, and was being dismissed like some importunate beggar. She looked down at the patient, and tried to think only of saving a human life.

'It's the carotid.' Leon was searching, his forehead furrowed, his breathing loud. 'Looks like a stab wound. Thank God it isn't severed. A stitch might hold it.' His voice was low and urgent. He reached for the artery forceps from the desk. 'Kerrie, hold this as tightly as you can. No time to get him to Theatre—he's got about two minutes if we can't stem this blood. I'll have to stitch it now!' He reached for his magnifying glasses and strapped them round his head. Kerrie stanched the bleeding, mopped the blood, and took the artery forceps from Leon, while he got his own needle and silk. Then he took over with the forceps, while she put sterile gloves on his hands one at a time. He handed her the forceps again. 'Try and keep the pressure on.' She was trying. If the artery was hidden by blood, there was no way he could find the torn part to sew together. 'Any sign of the duty doctor?'

'Rick was here. He would have helped.' But she said no more. She could understand Leon wanting nothing to do with a doctor who sent a patient away. He felt for the thin artery and put in the tiny needle more by feel than sight. He used the needle so delicately that it wasn't clear if he had actually found the bleeding vessel.

After what seemed an age, he said, 'Any pulse?' She could feel a weak pulse and nodded. 'I think I've got it. Let go slightly, and see if there's fresh bleeding.' She loosened her pressure on the side of the neck, rubbing her hands, which had gone almost numb. Very gently she swabbed the area. No more blood seeped from the vessel. Kerrie ventured to breathe a silent prayer of relief. Leon said, 'Would you get this blood cross-matched? He'll need about six pints. As quickly as you can?' He drew the skin together and stitched it neatly in place.

There was no need to ask. She knew how urgently a transfusion was needed. She ran to the lab, with a piece of soaked shirt. 'A stab wound—he's dying. Please hurry!' The technician analysed it, while Kerrie stood helpless. Then he took six packs of the correct blood-group from his fridge. Leon had already set up a drip and injected the needle into a vein. He attached the tube, and positioned the apparatus beside the couch. 'First time I've operated on an examination couch.' He straightened up at last, and pressed his hands into the small of his back. 'Now, let's take a look at the blood-pressure.' He took a reading from the other arm with his sphyg. 'We can get him up to Intensive now. He'll make it.'

They were suddenly alone together. All other feelings had drained away, and all Kerrie felt was total admiration for the way a man's life had been saved that night. 'I didn't think anyone could save him.' Her voice was tremulous, now that the emergency was over.

'It was touch and go.' Leon pulled off the gloves and mask. 'I'll just tell his friends they can come and see him tomorrow.'

Kerrie nodded. 'I'll get back.'

'No!' It was almost a command. Leon softened his toned. 'Don't go. Don't leave me yet.' And, although she didn't want any contact, she reacted instinctively to the pleading in his attitude. Strong he might be, a rock of safety to his patients. But underneath she could sense how he was feeling, how he had a desperate need for some form of release after the strain they had been through. She had seen other doctors after an emergency, and understood Leon's enormous relief, his need to be with someone who understood what he had done. Her body stood, longing to help him, while her mind told her she ought not to be there. Her body won.

He came back after talking to the patient's friends, and she saw his dark authoritative eyes as only weary and lonely now. He put his arm round her shoulders, loosely, and they walked together through the garden, loud as it was with the song of the crickets in the fragrant grass.

They were at his apartment door. Now was the time to leave. Now, in case anything happened that she would regret. But her body still acted as though it was the other half of his, staying close beside him, giving him its support and its warmth. They entered together, and clung together the moment the door had closed behind them. After a long time Leon murmured, 'He would have died if you hadn't helped me.'

'You saved him.'

'We did it together.' He kissed her lips, and the magic of last time was intensified by the emotions they had been through together tonight. He drew her gently, kissing her as they walked through to his elegant hall. 'Through there, Kerrie—you can get some of that blood off in there. I'll pour us a drink.'

She found herself in a pale blue-tiled bathroom, with a thick white carpet and towels to match. There were two blue towelling robes hanging up. She removed her stained dress and underclothes, and stood beneath the shower until she felt clean. Wrapped in a robe, she emerged, beginning to feel weary now, as the reaction set in to the flowing adrenalin of dealing with an emergency. Leon had brought a silver tray with tall glasses of something amber and sparkling. 'Drink that, you'll feel a lot better.' And he went into the bathroom.

Kerrie sipped the cocktail. It soothed her and filled her with a warm satisfaction at what they had achieved that evening. She sipped again, and had almost finished it when Leon came back, his dark hair sleeked back and his eyes looking relaxed again. He sat beside her on the sofa, his smooth body smelling of soap and of man. 'Thank you, my dear. Thank you for not leaving me alone.'

The wine had made her sleepy. 'Why didn't you let Rick help you?'

His voice hardened. 'Kerrie, you were there. You heard what he said to those poor people. He would have sent that man away to die. I don't find that very ethical, do you?'

'No, of course it was wicked. But you could have accepted his help when he offered it. God knows you needed it.'

'Maybe I could. Maybe I should have. But I'm not made of rock, Kerrie. I can't work with someone like that. I know what that man is, and I know he's making a play for you, that he thinks only of himself, and my God, Kerrie, it makes me so furious! I was afraid my anger with him would make my hand unsteady.' Leon put his hand to his forehead. After a while he said more calmly, 'So now you've seen me lose my cool. I'm sorry—a combination of saving a life I thought I'd lost, and of dealing with Rick O'Grady, whom I know to be one of the lower forms of life on this planet.' He reached out his hands and turned her round to face him. 'Can you still tell me

I'm being unfair to him? A doctor who can turn a dying man away?'

Her eyes searched his face. She had never seen him so agitated before. She said gently, 'No, not unfair tonight. He deserved to be despised tonight. But I think he honestly thought the man was dead. He'd lost so much blood.'

Her robe slipped from one shoulder, and Leon bent and kissed her shoulder, pressing his face against her neck, pulling her down further and further into his arms. 'Oh, Kerrie, if you hadn't been there——'

'I'm not going to——' Kerrie began to struggle. 'Have you no decency? What about Belle? You think she'd be happy to see us like this?'

He drew back, and his eyes were sincere. 'Belle Nader? Do you remember the afternoon we met, Kerrie?'

'Yes, I do—on the beach.'

'That afternoon we broke our—arrangement by mutual consent.'

'She still wears a ring.'

Leon nodded. 'I'm not surprised—she bought that herself. I never asked her to marry me. I think she only really wanted to be seen with me for the prestige it brought her.'

'Prestige? She's a good doctor in her own right, isn't she?'

'Very good, Kerrie. But you see, because someone in my past happened to be minor royalty, a lot of people see me as a sort of sultan myself. All wrong, of course, but that's what Belle is.'

Kerrie said thoughfully, 'Yes, she did manage to bring in the story of the princess.'

Leon smiled. 'It brought her aristocracy by association. But she grew impatient when I didn't commit myself, and that afternoon she told me she'd soon be leaving the Sultan if I didn't make our relationship official. Much to my relief. She won't be missed.' He drew her into his arms again, and this time Kerrie made no protest. The magic of their first kiss crept into her soul, and she couldn't push him away. Soon she was embracing him against her, never wanting to leave. They were drawn inevitably together. Tonight Kerrie at last lost the feeling of failure that Philip had inflicted on her. Tonight, in the sweet small hours of the night, there was nothing to make them separate. With her arms locked around his warm sinuous body, she knew she had wanted him like this the very first moment she saw him.

CHAPTER SIX

THERE were no operations next day. Kerrie worked quietly on the nursing wing, her mind on her work, yet sometimes wondering if last night had been a flight of her still-fevered fantasy. Had she really lain in Leon's arms, in a tangle of soft towelling and warm limbs, her cheek against his chest? And was it really Kerrie Snow who had crept from his arms in the first pale light of the soft pink dawn, and lain for a while on her own bed, filled with a tremendous sense of destiny? No one would guess, as the demure figure in its slim-fitting blue uniform moved on quiet feet round the wards, soothing, giving out medicines and advice, chatting to dear Mr Singh, who was soon to be discharged, and totally disregarding Sister Chan's crabby remarks as not worth worrying about.

'I hear you did some real heroics last night?' Kim, as usual, was first with the gossip.

Kerrie flushed, until she realised Kim meant the patient whose life had been saved. 'The professor performed spectacular vascular surgery on a patient on an examination couch. There wasn't time to get him to Theatre—it was a miracle he survived after the stab wound he had. I only held the artery forceps. Anyone could have done that.'

'Lucky you were on hand,' commented Kim.

'Yes.'

'You went out to meet Rick, didn't you?'

Kerrie laughed. 'What is it you really want to know, Kim?'

Joining in the laughter, Kim owned, 'Are you really getting serious with him? It looks as though he's quite keen—waiting outside for you like that.'

'If you're still thinking Rick O'Grady will eat me alive, forget it, Kim. He only wanted to offer me a job.'

Kim's face changed. 'Yes, that's what I was wondering. He's got his new premises, then?'

'Yes, he has—over the other side of town. No threat to the Sultan, I'd say.'

'Are you going to work for him?'

Kerrie thought about last night. They had worked closely together, she and Leon. In the euphoria of the moment, she had fallen into his arms knowing they were both free. It was fortunate that she had had the strength of mind to leave before either of them said anything they would regret. She said thoughtfully, 'My instincts would have been to go with Rick. I've always thought he was badly done to by the professor—until last night. I thought him a pleasant, open sort of chap. But I saw another side of him last night, a side that makes me think again.'

Kim was eyeing her doubtfully. 'You sound as though you haven't made up your mind.'

'Right. I'm confused at the moment. This is such a good job to give up.' They were on their lunch break, and Kerrie helped herself to salad. She couldn't tell Kim how her relationship with the chief had developed to something he might perhaps regret this morning. 'Has Rick asked you, Kim?'

'Yes, he has. But I can't see him paying as well as

the professor, in spite of the money he says he's borrowed from his wealthy sheep-farming uncle.'

Kerrie looked at her plate. So he had only offered Kim an ordinary job. Better say nothing about having the top administrative post. 'It's a bit of leap into the unknown. He says the place will be decorated and open in two months.'

'We have some time to decide, then.'

They were returning to the hospital when Kerrie's heart gave a leap in her chest, making her gasp. Kim said, 'What's the matter?' She looked up, and went on, 'It's only the prof. Why the drama?'

Kerrie tried to stay calm. 'Nothing.' She didn't want Kim putting two and two together.

Leon came closer to them. 'Good afternoon,' he greeted them. He was smiling, confident, most definitely the chief. Kerrie felt weak at the knees—that shiny dark hair she had actually kissed, and that tall frame she had embraced in the frenzy of passion. He stopped to speak to them. 'Kerrie, Dr Reza is coming tomorrow to look round the theatre. Will you be free to show him how our routine works?'

'I'll ask Sister.' Her voice seemed to come from far away.

'Good. And Kerrie—after the sterling service you gave that poor accident case last night, I'd like you to take the post of Sister yourself, right away. Would you see me in my office later?'

'Thank you.'

'You deserve it, Kerrie!' Kim was delighted for her friend, as Leon strode away. 'At least he's done the right thing, recognising that he couldn't have saved the man, but for you.' Kim chattered on, unaware how faint Kerrie felt at being openly spoken to in front of her friends in such a warm tone of voice. 'Does that make it difficult to decide now? Between staying here as Sister or going to Rick as nurse? You'd be crazy to leave now.'

'I know. This makes a difference.'

'Never mind. You don't have to decide this minute.'

'I think I do, Kim. It would be wrong to accept this promotion if I do have any idea of leaving. I've got some hard thinking to do this afternoon.'

Above them in a mango tree, two doves cooed affectionately to each other. The grass glowed green in the bright sun, and the hibiscus flowers were so vivid that they might have been painted on the bushes. Kerrie looked up, reminded of just how far away she had come from her parents' little seaside bungalow near the shingled shore. Yet emotionally, too, she seemed to have jumped from one crisis to another. Philip Wentworth—how long ago he seemed. How misty and far-away was her recollection of planning the wedding, making a list of presents, deciding who to ask to be bridesmaids. . . And now her heart was breaking for someone else. She knew she loved Leon da Cruz, yet couldn't fully give herself to him, while he retained in his heart this streak of vicious dislike of Rick O'Grady. Sure, Rick was no angel, as she noticed last night. But surely there was more than a simple clash of personalities here, each man hating the other. Leon had refused Rick's help with an insult. She must be destined to go through life with nothing turning out straightforwardly. Wouldn't it be safer to maintain her distance from all men for a while, especially Leon?

Reza was coming tomorrow; maybe she could request a transfer to Kalang Hospital for a while. It would be easier to make up her mind if she could be well away from both men. Lifting her chin, Kerrie marched into the cool of the nursing wing, and was delighted she was going to be kept busy, when Sister Chan gave her a string of jobs to do. Sister added curtly, after making sure Kerrie could repeat everything she had to do, 'I suppose you're very pleased to be promoted. You'll be able to answer me back when you're of equal rank.'

And Kerrie was amused to be able to reply coolly, 'I wouldn't dream of it, Sister. You're so much my senior.'

'I'm not so old,' retorted the other woman, nettled to be reminded that she was hitting forty.

'And you don't look it either, Sister Chan.' Soothing her ruffled feathers, Kerrie walked away to get on with her work. It might be nice not to have to work with such a cross patch!

Rick came briefly to the wards, to do a round of the minor ops he had carried out the previous day. Kerrie carried on taking temperatures and blood-pressures, but he managed a quick squeeze round her waist as he passed. 'How's my favourite administrator?' He whispered in her ear. Kerrie replied with a smile, and a nod towards Sister Chan, standing glowering in the doorway. Rick waited until Sister had gone, and added, in a low amused voice, 'No, I can't ask Chan—I only want pretty nurses in the Maharajah! Actually, I'm going round tonight to have a recce. Want to come along?'

'Not tonight, thanks. I need an early night.'

Rick turned serious. 'How long did you actually stay with da Cruz after I left?'

She said casually, 'You don't check your watch when you're clamping artery forceps round someone's carotid, Rick.'

'Don't play with me, Kerrie. Whose side are you on, anyway?'

'You know I've been on yours.' She looked up at him solemnly, knowing she had to tell him what she thought. 'You were unfeeling about that poor man, though—you know that. I was amazed that you wanted to send him away.'

'I honestly didn't think he had a chance.' Rick shrugged openly. 'Hardly any pulse. But I did offer to help.'

'You did, I know.' Kerrie knew her opinion of Leon had softened last night, and hardened slightly towards Rick. But he had offered to stay and assist, and it was Leon who had sent him away with anger and animosity in his voice. A rich and powerful man had no right to speak like that to a junior who was in no position to answer back, to dislike him enough to try and thwart his career. It still seemed fair to be on Rick's side over that. All the same, was it wise or sensible to carry her support for him as far as leaving a comfortable post at the Sultan for a new job that sounded great, but just might turn out to be a dangerous risk?

As Kerrie was leaving, the clock was striking six, and the evening was falling as it always did in

Malaysia, with astonishing speed. Suddenly it was dark, and the lights of Tajul were snapping on. Time to go and see Leon. She must stay only a moment. Last night was a special memory, but it mustn't happen ever again. They were both overwrought, and allowed their feelings to run away with them.

'Sister Snow?'

Kerrie turned at the door, to see a small, worried-looking Malay woman, in the traditional and rather expensive tunic and long skirt, with the scarf of the strict Muslim hiding her hair. 'Yes?'

'Oh, Sister, I thank you so very much! Professor da Cruz, he tell me how you help him save life of my son.'

Kerrie realised that she hadn't been to visit the patient in Intensive Care. 'How is he?'

'Please to come with me? He wish to thank you himself.'

Kerrie looked at her watch. Leon wouldn't mind; she knew how thoughtful he always was to worried relatives. 'Very well. What's your name? I'm afraid there was no time to take your son's particulars last night.'

'We are the Janar family.'

'The hotel owners?' Everyone had heard of the Janars. No wonder they had told Leon last night that the patient had money, and could afford to be treated at the Sultan!

'That is right. My son, he was attacked by jealous business rival. Thanks to Allah he did not die. I have no husband now, and I depend on my son to run the business.'

Kamal Janar was lying on his back, with the drip

still in his arm. But he was alert, and able to turn his head rather painfully and smile broadly at his mother. 'Kamal, this is nurse who help Professor do operation.'

The man's eyes were eloquent. 'I owe my life to you. My friends think last night I am dead, Nurse. I will never forget this thing that you have done.'

'It's only my job, Mr Janar—my duty.'

'My house is yours. If ever I can do a favour for you, only to ask.'

'Thank you. The best reward is seeing you getting better.'

After having her hands wrung fervently by Madame Janar, and further thanks from the son, Kerrie left them. She walked quite slowly now, unsure what she was going to say to Leon. While there was this doubt in her mind, she felt it only right to refuse promotion until she was sure she wanted to stay, and she must be brave enough to tell him why.

Across the floodlit gardens, where the small lake twinkled under spreading tamarind trees, and the tall palm trees towered into the stars, she walked, knowing she would regret it if she had to leave this lovely place, and not yet certain that it was the right thing to do.

Leon's door was ajar. He rose and came to meet her as soon as she tapped on it. 'I thought perhaps you'd forgotten.' He led her inside. 'Do sit down, Kerrie. Will you have a drink? Wine? Or maybe some fruit juice?'

'Not for me, thank you. You go ahead.'

He smiled at her. It was very hard not to respond. 'No, I'll leave it. Where were you?'

'I went to see Kamal Janar.'

'Ah, you found out his name. You know, I've actually met him socially. It was impossible to recognise him last night, he was in such a mess.'

'His mother is so grateful, I felt embarrassed. It's you they should thank.'

Leon sat down in a chair close to her. Now for it. She almost held her breath, praying that she wouldn't fumble her lines. She must make it clear right away that she might not be staying at the Sultan. Leon said, 'About last night——'

He had confused her. She had been expecting him to speak about her promotion. 'Oh—yes.'

Leon spoke in his gentlest voice, and its magic confused her even more. 'I honestly didn't mean things to go so far as they did. I was overwhelmed by you—by the emotionalism of saving a life that was almost certainly lost. You were part of it, and I didn't know myself just how much you've become to mean to me. I couldn't have saved that man without you, Kerrie, and at first I wanted only to hold you in my arms and thank you for being part of our triumph.' His words came more quickly now, and sincerity blazed from his beautiful eyes.

She said in a low voice, 'I think I felt the same. But you must have been in such a position many times.'

He reached for her hand then, and she stopped speaking, her throat constricting with sudden, unexpected tears. Leon said, 'Yes, of course I've come through serious operations before—saved lives before. But never with someone at my side who I feel so strongly about. That's why—things got out of hand last night—and why I want to say that I feel I must offer you marriage.'

'What?' The word echoed round her head. Marriage? How could she even think of him like that? And how dared he offer it as though it were a duty?

'I know there are vast differences in our backgrounds—there may be problems on that score,' he went on. 'And you also have been associating with a rather undesirable character. That will have to stop, of course, now that you know my feelings about O'Grady. But I intend to do the right thing, Kerrie. I've always faced up to my responsibilities. I'm willing to make you my wife. We have enough affection for one another, I believe, to make it work. Last night proved the warmth of my feelings for you.'

'But you don't understand——' This conversation was running away with her, and she had to stop it before it went any further. What embarrassing condescension! 'You're jumping to conclusions.'

'What conclusions, my dear?'

'That I would even consider marrying you.'

'But what choice have we? If it happens again—if there's a child——' His look was deep, almost tragic. 'My feelings are very strong, Kerrie. I know I want to make love to you. We must marry now, for both our good names.'

Kerrie stood up, gaining confidence from anger. 'Leon, I think what you've said is arrogant and patronising, and I find it very hurtful. Last night you were everything I could love. You were gentle,

Take 4 Medical Romances

Mills & Boon Medical Romances capture all the excitement and emotion of a busy medical world... A world, however, where love and romance are never far away.

We will send you 4 MEDICAL ROMANCES absolutely FREE plus a cuddly teddy bear and a mystery gift, as your introduction to this superb series.

At the same time we'll reserve a subscription for you to our Reader Service.

FREE

Every month you could receive the 4 latest Medical Romances delivered direct to your door postage and packing FREE, plus a free Newsletter filled with competitions, author news and much more.

And remember there's no obligation, you may cancel or suspend your subscription at any time. So you've nothing to lose and a world of romance to gain!

FILL IN THE FREE BOOKS COUPON OVERLEAF

Your Free Gifts!

Return this card, and we'll send you a lovely little soft brown bear together with a mystery gift... So don't delay!

loving, you seemed to need me and took pleasure from being with me.'

'That's right—I did. I do.' Leon reached for her hand again, but she drew it away. 'Kerrie, I didn't expect——'

She was breathing hard, as she tried to control her passion, and keep her voice low. 'As there's no child this time, as I have my period, I imagine you'd like to take back your proposal. I'll make sure it doesn't happen again. After all,' her voice was mocking now, 'my background is very humble compared with your grand ancestry. And I have unsuitable friends, according to you. Well, however unsuitable you think them, I have my principles too, and I don't think it right to be unfaithful to my friends—even on your advice, Professor da Cruz. For "both our good names"!' She wiped a tear from her cheek with the back of her hand. 'I'd better go.'

'No, wait.' Leon produced a silk handkerchief, and she took it, because the tears were threatening to mask her vision, and she didn't want to trip over anything when making her grand exit. 'Kerrie, please calm down. Don't go. I've not said things very well—forgive me for that; I've never asked anyone to marry me before. But don't go away in anger. Not after. . . Can't we talk quietly about this?'

She took a few breaths. 'There's nothing else to say, Professor. You've salved your family honour. I've said quite clearly that I don't wish to marry you. There's nothing else to say—except that I'd better offer you my resignation.'

'Resignation? But you can't—you have nowhere

to go. Kerrie, Kerrie, think again before you do something very foolish.'

Although he towered over her, Kerrie stood her ground, resentful of his superior tone, and spoke with all the dignity at her command. 'I have somewhere to go. I'm going to work for Rick.'

'My God!' Leon looked appalled, as realisation came to him. 'You mean he's got a place? I guess it's part of his dishonest nature that I'm the last to know. You'd be such a little fool to take a job with him. Why won't you listen to me and be warned?'

'Because, basically, I'm old enough to make my own judgements. He's taking me on as Administrator. And Rick doesn't patronise me. He treats me as an equal.'

Leon looked at her sadly. 'Then at least, Kerrie, this new hospital of his will be run efficiently. But you know so little about the man. I'd advise you not to rush into anything, just because I've annoyed you today.' There was a pause. He said, 'I don't want to lose you, you know. Even though you find me arrogant and patronising, I can be humble. Will you stay? I promise not to bother you again in your private life.'

His words twisted in her heart. 'I can't—I'm sorry. But I've made this decision now, and I think the best thing for us both is for me to make a clean break with the Sultan as quickly as I can.'

He said very quietly, 'If—there had been a child, would this still have been your decision?'

'Yes.'

'I had no idea you thought so badly of me.' When

she said nothing, he said, 'Would you have told me about the baby?'

'I don't know.'

'It would have killed me to know I had a child I couldn't care for.'

Kerrie turned away, aware that for both of them their closeness could prove their undoing. She could so easily have succumbed to his magnetism, the attraction which had seized her at their very first meeting. But she knew more about him now, knew that his perfection was flawed by arrogance, and that the only course for her was to put as much distance between them as possible, and as soon as possible. 'Goodbye, Leon,' she said.

And she was already several yards outside his apartment when she heard his reply, in his soft but authoritative voice, so used to being obeyed. 'I'm afraid that's not possible, Kerrie. Your work permit depends on your good conduct. If you leave the Sultan, you have no choice but to return to your hated Brighton, I'm afraid. I'll never allow you to go and work for O'Grady.'

Kerrie stopped and turned slowly to face him. He stood calmly at the door. She said, 'You'd really refuse me?'

'Yes.'

'It's—it's almost slavery, to keep me here against my will!'

'Call it what you like. I'm only thinking of you.'

'Can you explain why and how? Can you justify such meanness.

Leon put his hand to his forehead again, and she felt sorry for him even while hating his arrogance.

'No. Only that—that I know O'Grady better than you, Kerrie, and I know it's my duty to protect you from him.'

She shook her head miserably, knowing he had won. 'Call it your duty if you want to make yourself look less mean and jealous and vindictive. But I'll know your real nature now, and I'll never be able to think well of you again.' She walked across the lawn as quickly as she could. Just before she turned the corner and lost sight of him, she turned again. Leon was standing in the lighted doorway, and his face was in his hands.

She tried to slip into her flat without being seen, but Kim and Jami Arul were sitting in the hall, and they called out to her. 'Coming into town, Kerrie? We thought we'd try that new seafood restaurant to celebrate your promotion.' But then Kim saw her face and said quietly, 'Maybe you're not up to it, *lah*? You haven't been over your fever for very long.'

Grateful, Kerrie admitted, 'I do feel a bit tired.'

'Maybe we could bring you a take-away?'

'No, thanks. I'll have something in my room.'

She sat on the bed in the dark, thinking. Bitterness at Leon's treatment of her was mixed with a great disappointment that he could prove to be so jealously mean-spirited, when she knew how kind and thoughtful he was capable of being. Last night she had thought him the most perfect, most caring man in the world. What had happened? It all seemed to concern Rick O'Grady in some way. Yet Leon refused to say more. How was she going to manage to carry on working for him, after this?

She heard the phone ring in the corridor, and when no one answered it, she wiped her eyes again, and opened the door to the shadowy corridor. The phone still rang. She picked it up and cleared her throat. She heard Rick's voice saying, 'That must be you, Kerrie?'

'Yes.'

'I thought so. I saw you come out of da Cruz's place. You were crying.'

Kerrie clenched her fingers round the telephone. 'I don't want to talk about it, Rick, if you don't mind. Not tonight.'

'Can I come round for half an hour?'

'No.'

'Why not? We're mates, aren't we?'

She paused. 'Why doesn't he like you, Rick?'

It was Rick's turn to pause. After a while he said, 'Just jealous, I guess. He's a cold fish, you know, love.'

Kerrie knew differently. Leon had been ardent and warm towards her. Only the mention of Rick had turned him into a tense, heartless robot. Yet she recalled him standing in the doorway, his face in his hands, and she felt tears start in her eyes again. 'Leave it, Rick,' she said. 'I'll see you tomorrow. I don't want to talk now.'

CHAPTER SEVEN

THERE was a knock on her door. Kerrie mopped her eyes, and hoped they weren't too red. She had wept most of the night, and now it was morning, and she had to try to get back to work normally. She called weakly, 'Come in.'

It was Sister Chan. Kerrie sat upright, and tried to look businesslike. 'Sister, I was coming to explain——'

'There's no need—the professor has spoken to me. You are to be allowed to take some leave right away.'

'Are you sure you can manage?'

Sister Chan had never looked so aloof. 'We can get along very well without you, thank you.'

Kerrie turned and tried to bring herself back to real life. She hadn't seen Kim yet this morning. Kim would know there was something wrong. She felt she wanted to get away from here. Leon was giving her the chance of leave. Yet she felt very scared, suddenly. She had done what she thought was the right thing—yet it all felt wrong. Sister Chan said in a cold, harsh voice, 'The professor asked me to tell you there's no need to leave your apartment. I don't understand what's going on, but he says you're not under suspension, merely paid leave.'

'Oh, thank you, Sister.'

After Chan had gone, Kerrie felt very alone

indeed. Rick would be busy in Theatre. She must wait until the evening. It would all be all right then. Rick would sort things out for her. He would be able to get her a new work permit. Surely Leon couldn't keep her here when he knew she would be miserable?

She went to the dining-room for something to eat at lunchtime. The other girls came over, in ones and twos. 'Is it true you're leaving? Are you really going to take some time off for study?' So that was what Leon had told Chan to tell everyone. She was grateful for that. 'Do you think you're doing the right thing? We'll really miss you, Kerrie.' They were very nice. But when she asked if anyone else had accepted Rick's offer of work no one admitted to it.

Kim could tell that something was wrong. 'It isn't really study leave, is it, Kerrie?'

Kerrie shook her head. 'The professor and I have had a disagreement. I—I told him I wanted to leave, and he refused me permission.'

'I thought you were going to think it over.'

'I decided it was better to get it over at once.'

Kim said slowly, 'You're very brave, Kerrie. But maybe a bit reckless? Couldn't you apologise to the chief?'

Kerrie looked uncomfortable. 'I'm not going to— the argument was very bitter. But he's given me some time off to decide whether I want to stay on here or go home to England.'

'Go home? Oh, no, don't go, Kerrie. This will blow over.'

'And what do I do in the meantime? Sit in my room?'

It was a long afternoon. Kerrie didn't want to go out, in case Rick turned up wanting an explanation. It was quiet and lonely in the flat. She sat in the garden for a while. But when a rattling old van rolled up, and she saw Dr Reza and Polly get out and knock on the door of Leon's apartment, she pressed herself back against a tree-trunk until they went inside. In refusing Leon's proposal, she had also cut herself off from Kalang, and all the bustle of reorganising there. She had put in quite a lot of suggestions and ideas. It made her rather sad to think she wouldn't ever see how they turned out.

When it was late afternoon, and the sun was past its hottest, Kerrie decided not to wait for Rick any longer, but to go to his rented house in the main street and hope he was there. After all, she felt she had no choice now but to explain that she had burnt her boats at the Sultan, and hoped to work for him when Leon relented. And the sooner he knew it the better. She dressed simply, in a white pleated skirt and embroidered cotton top. The gardens were beautiful, as she skirted past the lake and disturbed a scarlet demoiselle crane. She would miss this place. But maybe it was time to move on. After her appalling row with Leon, it could never be the same here. She paused for a moment to look into the gentle lapping water—but the sound of a slamming door startled her and made her feel like an intruder, who ought not to be there, and she turned and hurried along the tree-lined alley that led to the main road of Tajul.

Rick's place was a modest little brick house, with a tiny garden containing a single papaya palm and some ragged grass. The front door, as with most Malay houses, was left open to make the most of any through breezes. Kerrie had seen the house from outside, but had never called before. Now she walked up the tiled path, and rang the bell.

There was a muffled oath inside. Then she heard Rick's voice, 'Coming!' In a moment he shuffled out of a darkened room in bare feet, wearing nothing but a pair of blue jeans which he was still buttoning.

'I'm sorry I disturbed you.'

'Kerrie, sweetheart, what a nice surprise!' But the words sounded forced. 'Say, love, can I catch up with you later? At the café, maybe? The thing is,' he lowered his voice, 'I've got someone with me.'

She wasn't jealous, but she did feel aggrieved at his lack of interest. 'I just came to explain—I've asked Leon to release me from my contract,'

'Say, that's great! Can't see him doing it, though—not if you told him about me! Look, can I buy you dinner on the strength of that? Meet you at the beach café where we had dinner last time, huh?'

'Very well. What time?'

'Make it. . .' He looked at his watch. 'Make it an hour. Say just after seven?'

'All right, I'll be there.' Kerrie turned, with a feeling of anticlimax. She had expected a bigger welcome than that. When she turned to look back, Rick had already gone back indoors. She walked slowly along the street. She had made her choice, one of the biggest of her life, and Rick wasn't even interested enough to ask her in. She went into the

Kentucky Fried Chicken house, and ordered a root beer. She could still see Rick's gates, and outside them a sleek Japanese car was parked. Could that belong to the person he had with him? She watched idly as the rush-hour traffic increased, then waned. The white Corona was still there.

Kerrie had almost lost interest, and was admiring the little Chinese shrine across the road, with lots of red candles and ribbons, and a lighted lamp sending off drifting puffs of blue smoke. Suddenly she heard the sound of an engine starting up. Bother—she hadn't seen who had got into the car. But she was in luck, as the car made a U-turn, and drove back right past the windows of the Kentucky Fried Chicken house. As she had expected, the driver was a woman. And she was an extraordinarily good-looking woman, with a confident Chinese face, and shining black hair piled up in glossy curls. It was a woman Kerrie knew—Dr Belle Nader.

Leon had said that their tentative affair had been ended on the day he first met Kerrie. Was Belle now flying to the arms of Leon's business rival in revenge? It certainly looked very much like it. Unless it was just business? Rick needed a consultant physician for his Maharajah, and Belle Nader would be quite a catch. Kerrie stood up, paid her bill, and began to walk slowly along the beach road towards the fish restaurant. It would never do for Rick to think she was spying on him.

Rick turned up right on time. He had been given time to compose himself, and he was once again the charming, thoughtful escort she had thought him on their first date. 'You look lovely, sweetheart. And

the news you came with made my day, believe me.'
And he held out a large bouquet. 'For you, my
sweet—the future administrator of the Maharajah!'

She accepted the flowers with a blush, as the other
diners were staring at Rick's extravagant gesture.
'That's jumping the gun a little,' she laughed. 'Leon
has refused to release me. I'm just hoping that in
time he'll see how mean he's being.'

He smiled and said calmly, 'Now don't worry.
Everything will sort itself out.'

'May I see the Maharajah some time?'

'Tomorrow—I'll take you along tomorrow. It still
needs a lot of work, though. Don't let it put you
off.'

'Even though I'm not allowed to work for you yet,
Rick, I thought maybe I could do a little informally—maybe advertise for staff? Three sisters, at
least three staff nurses——'

'I was thinking that we'd start off with two, love.'

'But—you don't mean only two shifts?'

'Well, yes, to begin with. We won't have a full
number of patients right away, remember.'

'Yes, but a twelve-hour shift! I can't see anyone
applying for that, Rick.'

He put his hand over hers and squeezed. 'There
you go! See how much I need you! Write down what
you think we'll need, and you have my go-ahead.
Informal—I like it, love! Old da Cruz thinks he's
got you under his thumb, and all the time you'll be
helping me start off on the right foot. You're some
sheila, you know that?'

Kerrie shook her head. The way Rick put it made
her sound underhand, and she didn't like that. But

what could Leon expect, after forcing her to stay at the Sultan? At least she could advise Rick, who didn't seem to have a clue about administration. 'Let's see how much accommodation you have first. Any caretakers in just now?'

Rick seemed not to know. 'Look, let's just enjoy our meal tonight. Start the hard work tomorrow.'

'All right.' She looked at her watch. 'I have to get back on time. Although I'm officially on leave, I'm still living in the nurses' home.'

'There's a top flat at the Maharajah, I told you I was thinking of using. It's yours, Kerrie, as soon as you can persuade da Cruz to see sense. We'll take a look tomorrow, and, if you like it, you can start planning the décor!'

Kerrie smiled at last. 'Oh, I knew you'd be able to sort things out. Thanks very much, Rick. I feel much better now.'

He felt in the top pocket of his shirt and brought out a bundle of Malaysian twenty-dollar bills. 'Here—first month's salary in advance. I reckon you might need it.'

'Oh, but——'

'Take it, Kerrie. I mean it.'

She shook her head. 'I'm still employed at the Sultan—it would be wrong. At the moment I'm only your unofficial part-time adviser and I want things to be above-board and honest.'

'Suit yourself, love. You're probably right; da Cruz could make trouble if he knew—even have you sent back to the UK.'

The waiter arrived with their *ikan kurau*, grilled golden brown, and for a moment they ate without speaking. Then Kerrie heard a low voice which was all too familiar. 'O'Grady, would you step outside for a moment? I think we have something to discuss.' Leon da Cruz stood at their table, immaculate in evening dress, his dark hair smooth as patent leather. 'You will excuse us, Kerrie?'

Rick looked up balefully. 'What do you want? Can't you see I'm eating?'

'Come outside. I don't want a scene.'

'Anything you want to say, say it. I'm not letting my fish get cold.' Rick cut a large chunk and forked it into his mouth.

Kerrie had stopped eating, her knife and fork poised, her appetite suddenly gone. Leon said quietly, 'Very well, if that's what you want. I learn that you've actually bought a place to set up on your own.'

'Too right, cobber.' Rick didn't look up.

'Then you're in violation of your contract with the Sultan, and I have the right to terminate it immediately.'

'Oh, sure, I forgot. Should have let you know. Anyway, I was going to leave tomorrow. You've saved me the trouble.'

'Won't you be warned, O'Grady? Don't you know what you're doing? How many more lives do you want to ruin?'

Rick placed his knife and fork on his plate and wiped the napkin over his mouth. Then he stood up. Leon was a tall man, but Rick was equally tall, and broad as well. Kerrie's palms began to sweat with apprehension. Rick said, 'I've just about had enough of you and your interference in my life! From now on, you stay out of my affairs, you stay out of Kerrie's and you stay out of my hospital. Any move to spoil the Maharajah, and you'll hear from my lawyers pronto. Get it?'

'I understand what you're saying, yes.' Kerrie could tell Leon was very angry, by the tense set of his head, the muscle moving in his jaw. Yet his voice did not rise, and she couldn't help but admire his self-control. 'You're aware that Kerrie still works for me? Maybe you'd have the courtesy to let me know how many more of my staff you're thinking of taking? And remember I also have lawyers.'

Rick allowed himself a small, triumphant smile. 'I'll let you know, squire.' He sat down again. 'Now, if you don't mind. . .?'

'You don't want to know how I found out about your *klinik*?'

Rick said casually, 'I guess Belle told you. She's got no loyalty for you now, you know. Better get used to that.'

Leon turned away, defeated. 'I'll be watching, O'Grady. One of these days you'll wish you'd started up your *klinik* a million miles from the Sultan, not just across town, where I can keep an eye on you.' For a moment he turned back and looked at Kerrie. She felt an impulse towards him, but knew her loyalty now had to be towards Rick and his new venture. All the same, her sense of honour made her feel uncomfortable, even though she was taking no money from Rick.

Rick called after the slim form retreating into the darkness, 'Don't hold your breath, Professor!' He looked across at Kerrie. 'Well, what do you think of your beloved Professor High and Mighty now? Is he a bastard, or what?' He drained his wine, and beckoned the waiter to bring more.

'I feel he's being unfair to you; I always thought doctors stuck together. And your place is miles away from him, on the other side of town. I can't see what he's making such a fuss about.'

'Just his jealous nature, Kerrie. Good job you found out in time what sort of guy he really is, huh?'

'Yes. Yes, you're right.' She had been offered marriage by that man. What a good thing she hadn't fallen into his arms, in purely physical response, but, instead, had listened to her reason, which reminded her that there could be no lasting happiness with a jealous, arrogant and unreasonable man.

'I'll take you back to the Sultan tonight, love. I'll pick you up tomorrow about five, and take you along to see my place, OK?'

'Oh, dear, it's going to be a long day!

'Spend the time planning my staff list for me, sweetheart. And don't forget, the nurses have to be pretty, and the cook has to be brilliant!'

'You're joking, aren't you? They wouldn't be my priorities in a new hospital.'

Rick smiled, and patted her hand again. 'Nor mine—just testing. You see now why I needed you so badly.' He leaned back and looked at her with amused, half-closed blue eyes. 'I just never imagined you'd want to come. I was sure there was something between you and the old professor. You gave me such a nice surprise when you turned up, Kerrie. You're a girl in a million, to stick up for me the way you did. You won't regret it, I promise you that. Da

Cruz can't hold you against your will for long, I'll bet on that.'

Just then, as the waiter cleared their plates away and took their orders for papaya ice-cream, someone else came to their corner table, and coughed politely behind her hand. 'Excuse me, but aren't you the English nurse from the Sultan?'

Kerrie turned to look at the slim, exquisitely-dressed woman with an elegant bearing and grey hair swept up into elaborate waves. A woman with money, that was for sure. 'Yes. At least, that's where I used to work.'

'You don't recognise me, Kerrie?'

Kerrie looked up directly into the thin, well made-up face, and dark intelligent eyes. 'It isn't—it can't be Madame Karela? Is it really? Oh, *madame*, you look so very much better!' and Kerrie stood to shake hands and kiss the old cheek, which had lost its papery texture, and glowed with health. 'I couldn't have believed it, you look so terrific. Oh. . .' she remembered Rick, 'You don't know Mr O'Grady. He used to be at the Sultan too, but he's starting up in a hospital on the Harbour Road, Rick, Madame Karela was one of my first patients.'

Rick rather ungraciously, stood up and bowed his head briefly. The old lady got the message. 'Well, I mustn't disturb you. But I shall always remember you, Kerrie. Here—my card. Whenever you have time, do come and see me.'

'I will, thank you.'

'That was Professor da Cruz with you earlier?'

'Er—yes. He had to go.'

'I thought I recognised his handsome face.'

Madame Karela smiled at Kerrie with a twinkle, and Kerrie's face burned as she remembered telling her about the two men in her life. This old lady was no fool. 'Give him my kindest regards when you see him. Goodnight, my dear. Goodnight, Mr O'Grady.'

Kerrie smiled ruefully at Rick, who tried not to sound grudging. 'It looks as though we'll have to change our restaurant, Kerrie,' he said. 'It's like a railway station in here!'

'I'm sorry, Rick, but I used to have long talks with Madame Karela. I had no idea she was so rich. Did you see those earrings?'

'I did, my dear. Maybe it's a good idea to go and see her some time. Recommend the Maharajah instead of the Sultan.' They both laughed—and Kerrie felt a twinge of conscience. Could she really recommend Rick, when Leon was by far the better surgeon? She hoped the situation never cropped up when she would have to make a choice like that.

As Rick drove her back to the Sultan, she wondered why he hadn't told her openly about Belle Nader. Kerrie had no intention of asking. But he seemed unusually coy about her—in fact, her name would not have cropped up if Leon hadn't turned up. When Rick did mention Belle, he used her first name, as though to emphasise to Leon that he had successfully poached, and was on first-name terms with one of his best doctors as well as one of his best nurses.

Kerrie opened the door with her latchkey, and tried to make no noise as she walked along the corridor towards her own flat. But as she opened the door she heard Kim's door open next door, and wasn't surprised when there came a gentle knock, 'Come in, Kim.'

Kim's voice was wistful. 'It seems a long time since we all used to go to the beach together.'

Kerrie nodded. 'I think I've aged about a hundred years.'

Kim, already cross-legged on Kerrie's bed, looked up at her. 'You don't look old. You look—sort of wise. You would have made a great sister if you'd accepted, you know. Someone the juniors could have come to with their troubles, not like old crosspatch Chan.'

'I know that. Don't rub it in. I would have wanted to stay if—Leon didn't make it impossible for me.'

'So you had dinner with the rival company! Well, I wish you luck, Kerrie, really I do. I hope things turn out well for you.'

'We might end up at rival hospitals, but we'll stay friends, won't we, Kim?'

'I hope so.'

The phone in the corridor shrilled and Kim ran to answer it before it woke up the entire apartment. 'Hello? Yes, she's here.' She handed the phone to Kerrie. 'Night Sister on Chan's ward.'

Night Sister was apologetic. 'I realise you're officially on holday, Kerrie, but we have an emergency admission, an old lady who says she knows you and is asking for you. Shall I tell her you'll come in the morning?'

'What's her name?'

'Moya Selim.'

Kerrie's thoughts flew back to the sunlit journey

through the Malaysian countryside, the first time she and Leon drove to Kalang Bahru. Old Moya, so full of gratitude to Leon for saving her life after a bad motor accident. 'Is she injured, Sister?'

'No. The professor has admitted her for surgery tomorrow. She's frightened it might be something serious.'

Kerrie said, 'I'll come at once.' She put the phone down, and said to Kim. 'A sweet lady I met in Kalang. I must go and calm her down.'

Kim nodded. 'Good for you, Kerrie. See you tomorrow.'

Little Moya seemed very small in the big white bed, and her dark eyes looked large and scared in her wrinkled face. Kerrie bent and kissed her cheek. 'You mustn't worry, Moya. You're in good hands here.'

'That I know. But I have such pain.'

'Has Sister given you anything for it?'

'Leon said I must not take anything. Operation is tomorrow early.' She reached out and clutched at Kerrie's hand.

Kerrie sat close, and stroked her brow gently. 'Try to sleep, my dear. I'll stay with you. Where is the pain?'

Moya pointed to her chest. Kerrie prayed it wasn't her heart. Gradually the old lady's eyes closed. Kerrie sat still until her breathing was regular. Her own eyelids were drooping, and she laid her head on her arms. Within a few moments, Kerrie too was asleep.

It was dawn when she woke, and found herself still at old Moya's bedside. The sky was a gentle rosy pink, and the birds in the tamarinds outside were trilling a welcome to the first rays of the sun. A calm, capable voice said, 'Good morning, Kerrie.' Leon was standing at the foot of the bed, with Moya's case-notes in his hands. He said, 'It was kind of you to come.'

Kerrie tried not to be affected by the sight of his noble face, the slim figure in the clean white coat. 'She asked for me. I couldn't let her down.'

'Actually I told her you were here. I realise you wouldn't be on duty—but I was hoping that in this case you might be willing to come to Theatre with her? I'd appreciate it if you would.' His eyes were gentle, as he looked down at Kerrie's tousled hair. 'You fell asleep, and I didn't want to wake you. Are you refreshed enough?'

So Leon had manipulated the whole thing! Kerrie looked at the sleeping woman, and forgot that she was annoyed with Leon. 'Yes, I'll help in Theatre. What's wrong with her? Not her heart?'

'I believe she has a pulmonary embolus. Would you prep her for Theatre and then come up with her? It would help her to stay calm, having you there. She took quite a fancy to you.'

Kerrie nodded. Did Leon know she had overheard Moya telling him not to let this one get away? 'I'll do it, of course. But I won't forget that you're keeping me here against my will.'

'I'm not likely to forget it either, Kerrie.'

'She will be all right?'

'She should make a complete recovery. Oh, by the way, Reza is here, you know. He'll be assisting me. I thought you might like to have a cup of coffee with Polly, and a bite of breakfast?'

'Thanks, I will.' She walked past him into the corridor, feeling the warmth of his breath on her cheek as she unavoidably brushed against him. 'Shall I prep the patient now?'

'Please. I'll see you in Theatre, then.'

'Yes, Professor.'

'You couldn't make it Leon?'

She turned and looked into his eyes. 'I don't think so. Not at the moment. It wouldn't be right.'

'Kerrie, I——'

'Excuse me, Professor, but I have to go for the gown and the prep tray.' She escaped before things became too personal. If Leon tried, he could be very persuasive.

CHAPTER EIGHT

DURING the operation Kerrie kept her eyes firmly fixed on her tray of instruments. She was well aware of the magnetism of Leon's dark brooding look, above the mask, and equally determined not to allow his physical presence to undermine her intention to continue to press for release from her contract. She watched his skilled fingers as he located the embolus which was clogging a vessel in the old lady's lung, and removed it, allowing the blood to flow again. 'Would you mind suturing, Reza?'

'Not at all, Chief.' Reza started to close the wound, while Leon strode from Theatre, already beginning to strip off his gown and gloves. Kerrie kept her gaze on the suture, and pretended she didn't care if Leon came or went. Reza said, 'You'll stay with her, Kerrie? It's always better when there's a familiar face when the patients come round from anaesthetic.'

'Of course I will.'

Reza said, 'I'm glad we meet again, Kerrie. Leon led me to believe that you were on holiday.'

'I am. I only came in because I know Moya, and she asked for me.'

'Well, I'm delighted. I hope you'll have lunch with Polly and me—this is, if you're not busy.'

It was impossible to refuse this cheerful man

anything. 'I'm not doing anything till later in the afternoon.'

'That's great.' Reza snipped the silk at the end of the wound. 'There. Can you take this patient to Recovery, please?'

Polly was welcoming too. 'When are you coming back to Kalang Bahru?,' she asked. 'It was fun while you were there—until you caught fever, that is. You would be so pleased with the improvements.'

Leon, tactfully, didn't join them for lunch. Kerrie felt sad that a promising friendship couldn't develop with Polly and Reza, because of her feelings of antagonism towards Leon. It was with slow footsteps that she dragged herself away from their cheerful lunch table, calling in on Moya before going back to the flat to shower and change in time to meet Rick O'Grady as she had promised.

Rick kept up a stream of banter as they drove through the centre of town, and across to the east side. The cheeriness was useful, as it hid Kerrie's own sadness. Kerrie wasn't familiar with this part of town, and became more and more silent, as they passed dilapidated warehouses, narrow littered streets, and a smelly street market selling cabbages, shoddy toys and bunches of overripe bananas. It was three in the afternoon, and the smell from stale fruit and rotting vegetables filled the warm heavy air between the high storehouses and shadowy shops.

She could see the sea, sparkling and bright, in small patches between the buildings, and could smell the salt, fishy smell that proved they weren't far from the fish market. Occasional high brown sails moved sedately by, as the fishing boats came in to land their cargo, and hordes of screaming gulls swooped in to 'assist' the unloading.

When Rick braked, and brought the car to a stop beside an empty monsoon drain, Kerrie looked about her in disbelief. They couldn't have arrived at the hospital yet. They were still among the warehouses, on the narrow cobbled street. But he said, 'This is it! Just look at that view, Kerrie!' and pointed out to sea.

But Kerrie looked back, at the squat brick building with white paint coming off in large flakes, and windows without glass covered with rotting shutters. 'This?'

'Don't look so disgusted, Kerrie! You haven't seen inside yet.' He led the way to the entrance, which was closed by high wooden double doors. A group of ragged children looked on with wide eyes, and a couple of street traders watched them more covertly.

As her eyes got used to the dimness inside, Kerrie realised it had once been quite a grand house—maybe the harbourmaster's, or a Customs officer's. Rick was eyeing her cautiously. She looked at him and said, forcing herself to be hearty. 'I can see what you mean, Rick. It has possibilities. But it will cost the earth to decorate.'

'That's no problem, because I got the building at a knock-down price—plenty left for the transformation. See, there's even a garden—a good gardener could put in a few shrubs and flowers—put up a white fence to keep the local dogs out, and already you can see a difference. Come up to the flat, and you'll see what I mean.'

It was a wide staircase, once gracious, but now the wood was soft in places, which even a carpet couldn't hide. 'The first floor will be the operating theatres,' said Rick. 'Wards on the ground. And *voilà*—the penthouse apartment!' And up a narrower staircase was the top floor. 'Now isn't that view something?'

Kerrie nodded. The view was splendid—right over the marina, with its fishing boats alongside pleasure cruisers and launches that took visitors out to see the islands a mile or so out in the brilliant South China Sea. Palm trees bent low over the water in places, and flowering bushes gave the outlook vivid splashes of colour. She swallowed, and said, 'It could be worse.'

'This will be the bedroom.' He opened a door into a room with bare boards for a floor, and walls painted a sickly shade of sea-green. 'No need to cook when you move in—see down there? A great little Chinese restaurant.'

'Is there a bathroom?'

'There certainly is. Complete with water heater.' And again Rick led the way along rickety boards. The bathroom was in fair order, but the white bath, lavatory and basin were covered with a fine layer of dust. 'You take your time looking around. Just imagine what this will be like in a couple of months.' He clambered up to the top floor.

Kerrie tried. She tried very hard indeed. If the entire wooden superstructure was replaced with fresh wood and new shutters, the walls painted pastel colours, and the place furnished with decent beds and chairs, it would pass as a reasonable hospital. But the amount of equipment needed was staggering.

And then she saw the rat. It was sitting on its hind legs, cleaning its whiskers. Kerrie didn't scream. For a moment she didn't move. Then, carefully, she drew her shoulder-bag towards her and walked very deliberately out of the building. She beckoned to a passing trishaw. 'Take me to town, please.'

'OK, *lah*.'

Kerrie dialled the Sultan from a hotel in the main street. 'Is Mr O'Grady there?'

'I'll check for you.' Kerrie waited. The girl came back. 'Hello, caller. I cannot find Mr O'Grady at the moment. Can I give him a message?'

'Please. Tell him Miss Snow is at the Morib Hotel for the next couple of days.'

'Very good.'

Kerrie leaned back in the hotel lounge, suddenly realising how tired she was at the events of the day. It wasn't the end of the world, finding that Rick's dream hospital was still in the embryo stage. She could continue with her leave, staying in town so that she didn't run into Leon, and had some time to think over whether she really wanted to go ahead and work for Rick.

The next thing she knew was waking up, that it was very dark, she could see a full moon through the hotel window, and someone was speaking her name very gently. Rick! But Leon da Cruz stood there, and she knew she was glad to see him in spite of trying to get away from him. She said coolly, 'I suppose the telephonist told you I rang Rick?'

'Yes, she told me. I was worried about you. Why

come here? Why leave the Sultan flats? At least you have friends there.'

She shook her head. 'Can't you understand? I had to get away. It feels like a prison there.'

'May I sit down?' She nodded, and he sat in one of the easy-chairs beside a low table. Kerrie sat down opposite to him, on the edge of the chair. Leon leaned forward, his shoulders smooth and broad in the silk shirt. 'I'll be frank. You want to leave my hospital, and you refused my offer of marriage. But that doesn't mean we have to be enemies, Kerrie. In fact, I admire you for your loyalty to that—that O'Grady fellow, and I admire your courage. So please, if you need anything, let me help?'

It sounded so eminently reasonable. She had been feeling lost and bewildered, but Leon's easy commonsense and tact gave her back her sense of security and calm. She said apologetically, 'I was rude to you, I'm afraid. I didn't like doing it, but you deserved it, you know.'

He smiled slightly at her admission, and she was reminded of the first time she had met him on the beach, and how the smile lit up his eyes. 'Not rude—outspoken.'

'I was expecting Rick.'

His eyes were hooded. 'I know. But he isn't working there any more, and I don't know where he went. Maybe if you try his home?'

'Why are you helping me? There's no need, honestly. I don't want to be a trouble to you.' At his look, she knew there was no need to worry. He wanted to be here. She went on, 'I wanted to get away from the Sultan for a while.'

'I can understand that.'

'Rick drove me down to look at his new place.'

'You don't have to explain if you don't want to.'

'I ought to tell you what happened. You see, he was showing me this house, and there was a huge rat—and I ran away.'

Leon nodded. 'So you wanted to find Rick to explain why, and you rang the Sultan instead of his lodgings. And by now he's probably gone out for something to eat. Why don't we do the same thing? You must be hungry by now. Come on, give your face a rinse and brush your hair. There's the ladies' room. Don't stay here all alone, Kerrie. It doesn't make sense.'

She obeyed him as though her own will wasn't working. He was right; she could do no good waiting here. She washed vigorously, and did her hair neatly, even put a little lipstick and blusher on. It made her feel better.

She knew very well that other women were watching her enviously, as Leon turned and smiled, and walked forward to meet her. They stopped, facing each other, and she felt a surge of that same longing that had driven them into each other's arms that first day in Kalang. They must look, to the outside world, like two lovers meeting. Kerrie felt her face growing pink, and was the first to look away. Leon took her arm gently and steered her towards the dining-room. 'You won't want to go out, with so much on your mind. Let me just see you eat a decent meal, then I'll leave you in peace.'

Peace! If he wanted to give her peace, he ought to release her from her contract. Her heart was getting very little peace, at his closeness. But she knew he was right, that she must eat properly, and go back to the Sultan in a couple of days, and work normally until things were sorted out. Leon perhaps knew what he was doing, making her stay on. Rick wasn't proving a very reliable friend.

He ordered for her. Usually decisive, Kerrie's mind was elsewhere. Anyway, Leon knew what to order from the vast and delicious menu, and soon they were sampling bowl after bowl of savouries, with their chopsticks, Kerrie only then realising that she was ravenous. 'I must have this meal put on my bill, Leon,' she said firmly. 'I'll be staying here for a night or two.'

He looked up from a tender piece of Peking duck. 'I won't argue with you tonight, but it goes against all my feelings of chivalry!'

'You've been chivalry itself. Thank you, Leon, I appreciate it.' She took a sip of Chinese tea. Feeling bolder, she asked, 'Could you tell me why it is you're so much against anything Rick O'Grady does? Were you ever friends? You must have thought him a good surgeon, if you employed him at your hospital.'

He nodded, his face grave. 'We were on good terms once. I can't go into details, but he let me down. He caused me a lot of heartache. I know that he thinks I'm wicked, to try to thwart all his plans. I also know that he paints me as a black-hearted villain to anyone who'll listen.'

'Why can't you go into details, when it matters so much to me?'

'Kerrie,' he laid down his chopsticks for a moment as he looked at her with an anxious frown, 'if anyone could get me to speak it would be you, but I've given my word. I'm sorry.'

She shrugged. 'So I'm to believe he's the bad guy? How can I judge if you won't tell me why? I have to go by what I know of him, don't I?'

'I know—and I respect you for it. I once warned you to steer clear of him. You asked me not to say it again, and I respect that too. You must live your life your way. But forgive me if I keep half an eye on you, to make sure you never get hurt.'

'You're very kind, Leon—kind to everyone except poor Rick. I just can't understand. You treat him as though he didn't really belong to the human race.'

His expression was rueful, as he picked up his chopsticks. 'Come on, Kerrie—don't leave all this to go to waste!' She obeyed. After a while, Leon said, 'If you don't want to come back to the Sultan right now, would you care to go up country? They could make good use of you at Kalang. I wouldn't be there to get in your hair. Reza and Polly would be delighted, you know. And, as far as I know, they haven't got a rat problem!'

'Are you sure?'

'Very sure. Interested? The theatre is taking shape nicely.'

She nodded slowly. 'Interested, yes. And thank you. Can I let you know in a day or two?'

'Of course you can.' He leaned back in his seat.

'That wasn't bad, was it? Now, what are you going to choose for dessert? I hear the banana splits are famous here.'

'I couldn't possibly!' She was laughing, as someone came over. She looked up—and it wasn't the waiter at all, but Madame Janar herself. '*Madame*, don't tell me this is one of your hotels?'

The little woman was dressed in a long Malay skirt and tunic in glittering blue fabric, and a white scarf was draped round her head and shoulders. 'Good evening to you both. How lucky I am to have the chance of thanking you again for your great skill that saved my son.'

Leon shook his head. 'Enough thanks, *madame*. It's quite enough to see the smile on your face.'

'Professor, Nurse Snow, I am happy you have chosen to eat here. You will eat here without payment for the rest of your lives.'

They both protested, but Madame Janar insisted, and she knew how to get her own way. When she learned that Kerrie was thinking of staying at the hotel, she insisted she could stay as long as she liked as her guest. 'And you must have the best room.'

After she had gone, Leon said, 'Well, you'll be more comfortable here than in Kalang, I suppose. But the offer stands. Say the word, and I'll send a driver for you.'

'Shall I call you tomorrow, as soon as I can?'

'Good.'

It was late when he looked at his watch. 'You know, Kerrie, when you left my apartment like a beautiful whirlwind that night, I thought you were

going out of my life. I'm glad you let me in again—
even just a little.'

Again they exchanged a look, saying nothing, and
again Kerrie's heart ached for him, as she was the
first to lower her eyes. 'You won't—do anything to
stop Rick opening his hospital?'

He didn't answer immediately. He seemed to be
searching for the right words. 'I'll do what I think is
right. And I'll try to make sure nobody is hurt when
I do it.' And he stood up, bowed slightly, his eyes
looking deeply into hers, and in a moment he was
gone.

She sat for a while, staring into her coffee till it
grew cold. Then she rose, and went slowly to the
desk. The desk clerk smiled. 'Miss Snow, please
come this way.' And he led her to a spacious
apartment, with a sitting-room, luxurious bathroom
and dressing-room. 'Madame Janar insists you use
this suite as long as you wish, with her compliments.'
He was noticeably polite to her now, insisting on
taking her order for breakfast, and wishing her a
good night's sleep. In her amusement at his grovelling, she forgot how empty her soul felt when Leon
left her alone.

She waited until almost midnight before she tele-
phoned Rick again. There was still no answer.
Kerrie went to bed, still anxious about Rick, but
luxuriating in the perfect atmosphere, the deep
warm comfort of the large bed. There was even a
choice of taped music, as well as a complimentary
bottle of wine, a large bowl of fruit, and some
beautiful spider orchids in a crystal vase. She
switched on a gentle lullaby of light music. She

would decide what to do in the morning—if she
managed to get hold of Rick. She imagined him
searching the area, questioning people round the
harbour and marina who might have caught a
glimpse of her leaving the pathetic hulk of the
Maharajah Klinik.

Breakfast was served in her sitting-room. She
wore her flowered cotton housecoat, and thought
how simple it looked in that grand suite. But the
scrambled eggs, the golden toast and fresh butter
took her attention, and she was concentrating on the
last cup of coffee when her telephone rang. She
picked it up. 'Yes?'

It was the desk. '*Madame*, there is a gentleman to
see you—a Mr O'Grady. Do you wish me to direct
him to your suite?'

'Oh, yes, please.' It would have been nice to have
a shower first, and dress in that lovely dressing-room
with its long gilt mirrors and elegant vanity units.
But Rick mattered. The sooner they discussed their
plans, the better.

He was wearing trousers, and a real shirt, though
with no tie. The name of the Morib Hotel must have
made him tidy his outdoor image up a bit. 'Good
morning, Rick. I've been trying to reach you at
home.'

He didn't smile. 'Da Cruz rang. I suppose this
swanky room is your way of telling me what I can do
with my hospital?'

'Rick, please sit down, and listen to me.' He sat,
grudgingly, and she poured him a cup of coffee from
the silver pot. 'I ran away after I saw a rat. I was
terrified!'

'I realise that—I'm sorry. I found the trishaw wallah who took you into town. He said you were shaking.'

'Well, I booked into here because it was the nearest. I only meant to stay until something else turned up. The reason I've got this suite is that the owner is a patient of Leon's, and she wanted to show me how grateful she was, that's all. Now, tell me about the plans. How soon can you get the Maharajah operational, and when do you think it would be a good time to start advertising for staff?'

Rick's face brightened. 'Well, that's beaut talk, Kerrie. Thought you'd never want to come back. I thought da Cruz would have lured you back by now. He's done his best to turn you against me.'

'That's what he said about you.'

He sipped the coffee. 'I was—er—talking most of the night with a friend who's going to help. In fact, if we go along now, I guess the builders and decorators are already in.'

'So it won't be long?'

'Coupla weeks before you need to do anything.'

'Couple of weeks.' Kerrie looked thoughful. 'Leon won't have released me by then. Maybe you'd better go ahead without me, Rick. I'm more of a liability now.'

She expected him to be suspicious of that, but he said cheerily, 'You don't know how glad I am that you'll be one of the team eventually, Kerrie. I'm full of confidence now.'

'I thought you always were confident. The type of man who breezes through life.'

He turned towards her with a wry grin. 'That's the

effect I like to give. But, inside, you'd not recognise the nine-stone weakling! I've been through some toughies, Kerrie. It hasn't been an easy ride.' He reached for her hand and drew her close, putting his arm round her waist and hugging her. 'Thanks for sticking by me. Guys like me need all the real friends we can find.'

She looked up at the blue eyes, at the curly fair hair. 'It hasn't been an easy ride.' Leon had said something similar. She stroked his head lightly. 'Maybe one day you'll tell me the story of your life, Rick?'

He grinned again. 'Not for the delicate stomach, sweetheart.'

'But why? You did know Leon some time ago, didn't you?'

'What's the guy been saying about me?' Rick's voice became tense and suspicious.

Kerrie was soothing. 'Nothing at all. He said he's given his word and couldn't tell me anything.'

'That's a change, anyway. I'll tell you one day, Kerrie, my love, and that's a promise. My word on it, and I can be just as honourable as bloody da Cruz, I tell you, kid!'

Kerrie frowned slightly. Sometimes her future employer could sound quite coarse. She was relieved to see him go. After Leon's kindness today, she knew she was beginning to rethink her decision to get away from him. She had been quick to cast him in the role of villain to Rick's golden-haired hero. But the more she learned of the two men, the more undecided she became.

As though she couldn't stay away, she took a cab

to the Sultan that afternoon, officially to visit Moya Selim. But she knew she also wanted to see some of her friends, and maybe even catch a glimpse of Leon da Cruz. He had proved himself a good friend, now that he had dropped his foolish idea of marrying her for the sake of his honour. Helpless, she knew she wanted to talk to him again; that Rick O'Grady had talked a lot, but had not given her the reassurance she still needed to make up her mind.

CHAPTER NINE

THE morning was sweet, the sky delicate pink, and the palm trees graceful against the sky. As she swam lazily in the shallows, basking in the sun's warmth, Kerrie felt guilty for relaxing when others in the Sultan would be working hard. It wasn't fair to go on with this holiday idea. She was still employed by Leon da Cruz, and, while he would not allow her to terminate her contract, she might as well go back to work, if he would allow that at least. Soon she might have a job they would all envy. She knew that was a decision still to be made. But right now Kerrie knew she wanted just to get back to the ward, and to her patients, and she hoped very much, as she rubbed herself dry with the beach towel, that Sister Chan would be forgiving enough to take her back.

Rick hadn't been in touch. He had a lot on his hands, preparing the new hospital for its bright new future. Kerrie tried to be understanding. She thought of the rat, and of the cockroaches in the kitchen, and gave a shudder.

She walked up the sand and lay on her towel in a shady place under the trees, where bushes and scrub between the palms made it quite private. Closing her eyes, as she gathered up her courage to ask if she could start work again, she tried not to think of Leon, and of their disturbingly turbulent relationship. Last time they had talked, he had been calm, controlled—and so kind. His was a puzzling nature. Superbly gentle he was, with his patients and most of his staff. Yet with Rick O'Grady there was so much irrational dislike that it was hard to understand. Rick was such an open and cheerful person; how could anyone dislike him to such an extent? True, she had discovered another, harsher side to his happy-go-lucky nature, but it wasn't enough to make an outcast of him, surely?

Kerrie's eyes were still closed. She wasn't asleep, but not really awake either. It was almost a waking dream, when she heard voices not far away from her along the beach; a man's voice, and quiet oriental woman's reply.

She opened her eyes just a little, and almost gave herself away by gasping at the sight. A tall man was laying out a cloth for a woman to put her basket on. It was almost history repeating itself, because the woman was Belle Nader, in a loose, flowing beach wrap. The man, however, though tall, was also broad and fair-haired—Rick O'Grady! He was saying, 'Where do you want this, sweetheart? Strewth, what have you got in here? It's weighing me down!'

And Belle looked up and laughed her tinkling, artful laugh. 'Nothing weighs you down, Rick. Don't pretend. Anyway, I brought some beer—I know your favourite brand now.'

'You're a doll, you know that? Spoiling me like this.'

'Well, we can't do any good hanging around your Maharajah, can we? We'd get in the workmen's way.'

They moved closer together among the bushes, and Kerrie heard nothing clearly. Then Rick stripped off his shirt and jeans and ran down the beach into the sea in striped cotton shorts. Kerrie, still flat on her back, turned her head slightly to see Belle. The woman was smiling to herself, and, beautiful though her face was, the expression on it reminded Kerrie of that of a crocodile who had just enjoyed a good meal. She turned away quickly. She had never taken to Belle. She had believed it was hidden jealousy because Leon had been almost engaged to her. But now, somehow, she had the feeling that Belle Nader couldn't really be trusted.

Kerrie's problem now was to get away before she was seen. Obviously, from the picnic basket, the other two would be down here until afternoon. She lay rigid, praying she wouldn't be discovered. Then she heard Belle giggle as Rick came running back, dripping wet, and flung himself down beside her, scattering her with sea water. Belle said, 'Where did you say Kerrie Snow is?'

'Staying at the Morib Hotel. Why, love?' Kerrie heard the rustle as he pulled Belle down on top of him, and her squeak at his wetness. 'She won't be any bother. I told her I'd get in touch in a coupla weeks.'

Belle's voice was serious and thoughtful. 'I didn't expect her to be willing to leave Leon da Cruz. Strange girl. I believe she might be falling for you, Rick. She certainly came down on your side. You shouldn't really neglect her for two weeks, if you want to keep her loyalty.'

'Honey, are you sending me away from your

irresistible body? I gave up on that young lady when she told me her boyfriend had called off the wedding. There's only one type of woman who gets that done to them, and that's the frigid type. I want nothing to do with that, Belle—you know my passionate nature. I could tell, the minute I touched her, and felt her tense up.'

'She could have just got wind of your reputation, my dear.'

Rick laughed, and there was a lot more rustling. His voice was deep and satisfied. 'Darling girl, what do I want with little nurses when I've got a real woman at last?'

There was the sound of a can being opened, the ring pull jerking off with a fizz. 'Here, big boy, have some Tiger beer. It'll keep you cool and occupy your hands for a while. I want to rest.'

And then Rick's voice became indistinct, as they murmured together. Kerrie heard only fragments. 'Da Cruz—a cold fish—in bed—warm-blooded Aussie—real thing. . .'

And Belle, saying with a throaty laugh, 'Forget him. His money was the best thing about him. Wait till we start taking his patients! Hit him in his wallet. . .'

Kerrie rolled over, hating Belle Nader. How dared they say he was a cold fish? Leon was warm and passionate and desirable. She hated the lies they were spreading about Leon more than she disliked being talked about herself. It was quite clear now where Rick had been, the night she couldn't find him at his home. He was spending the night with Belle Nader, who was putting her own money into the Maharajah—and providing Rick with rather more than just financial comforts. At least Rick was being honest about Kerrie. It wasn't very flattering, calling her frigid, but at least he was straight, not cool and calculating, like Belle was.

To her immense relief, a family with several children came down to the beach and positioned themselves between her and the other couple. To the cheerful shouts of the children, she quickly collected her towel and beachbag, pulled on her cotton jeans and T-shirt, and ran up silently among the trees.

She stopped at the path that led up to the Sultan. How she missed the other girls, all the fun they'd had, sharing their days off, picnicking and swimming, and gossiping among the trees. For old times' sake she wandered along the path and through the gate, and stood for a long time, hidden by the shrubbery, gazing at the lovely gardens of the Sultan, with their atmosphere of serenity and timelessness. Was she really so clever, giving up all this? Even when the Maharajah was finished, it would only have a tiny garden. Where would she go for privacy and for friendship? She sat down on the grass for a while, her back against a tall coconut palm, wondering what kind of replies they would get when they advertised for staff. Would any of the nurses be as much fun as the ones who had become her good friends here?

Just then a door opened and someone came out in surgical green. The replacement for Rick, maybe. But as soon as she saw the shining dark hair, and the noble set of the head, she knew it was Leon, and pressed herself back against the tree trunk, so as not to be seen. He was walking along the walkway from the hospital wing to his own apartment, and with him was a woman Kerrie didn't recognise. They were chatting in low voices, and she saw Leon turn at something the girl said, and give her that slow smile, his eyes appreciative. It stung Kerrie like a sharp sword. That was the man who had asked her to marry him.

And then two nurses came out, laughing, and by their light step it was obvious they were coming off duty. Kerrie started to get up to go, but one of the girls saw her, and shouted, 'Kerrie! Hey, don't go!'

She stood up then, and waited for Kim and her friend. 'Hi.'

Kim stopped, waving to her friend, who went on to the nurses' home. 'I wouldn't mind a swim.'

'I was just going in, Kim, if you don't mind. I've decided to ask Chan for my leave to be cancelled. I'm bored doing nothing when you're all working hard.'

Kim smiled. 'I'm sure she'll have you back. That's good news. See you later, then? Come over and eat with us—no one will mind. How's the new place coming on?'

'Don't be so understanding, Kim. Call me a pig— I won't mind. I feel a bit like a traitor, you know.'

'Don't say that! No one blames you for wanting a better-paid job. It's only sensible.' They went into the dining-room and were soon sitting at their old table, eating *wanton mee* and drinking diet cola, as though Kerrie had never been away. Kim said, 'The new hospital isn't quite as good as you thought?'

'How did you know?'

'By your face, Kerrie. I've never seen you look quite so grim.'

Kerrie smiled. 'I've just heard Belle Nader talking to Rick. Sounds as though they're partners.'

'Well, come on—tell me all about it!'

In between chopsticks of *mee*, Kerrie told Kim everything—the rat in the horrible flat, about Rick and Belle Nader, and about how lonely she felt when she heard them talking about her on the beach. 'There, now I've got that off my chest, there are some good points. Rick won't be harassing me now he's in love with Dr Nader. I just wish I'd never said I'd like the job now.'

Kim's face was sympathetic. 'But you said you were asking to be released from here on a matter of principle. Everyone thinks you're quite brave and independent.'

'Not foolhardy and stupid, then?'

'No, honestly!' Kim was smiling, but it was a nice friendly smile, and Kerrie was already feeling better.

Kerrie said, trying to be casual, 'How's the professor?'

'Fine—in quite a good mood today. I think his new secretary helps. She's very quiet, but she's very bright. He likes talking to her. They get on well.'

'I think I saw her—going to his apartment.'

'Could be. They both like classical music.'

Kerrie said with a touch of irony, 'Music, eh? A lunchtime concert?' She had to say something light, to ease the burst of violent jealousy that made her cheeks burn and her throat go dry.

'Well, she's only been here a few days! Anyway,

the professor is leaving soon for a lecture tour of Europe. Some of the girls think it's because of Dr Nader's leaving. I don't think that. I never thought they were well suited at all.'

Kerrie didn't answer. How could she tell anyone in the world that Leon had left Belle ages ago? It was a secret Leon had told only to Kerrie. She looked down for a moment. Now she was the lonely one, while Belle amused herself with Rick, and Leon quite clearly wasn't missing her one bit. Kim said, 'I'm off this afternoon. After you've seen Sister Chan, we could see a film and have a meal out. What do you say.'

Kerrie nodded eagerly. 'Sounds wonderful. Just what we need. And Kim—thanks.'

'Sure.' Kerrie waited for Kim to change out of uniform, then they walked along the boulevard beside the sea, towards the harbour. It was over three miles, but the breeze was kind, and they were young and fit. They watched the fishing-boats, and the ferry to the islands. There were some sleek racing yachts out practising, making a brave sight as they swept smoothly over the glittering waves. As the two girls came to the less salubrious streets, Kerrie felt she had to explain. 'It's a bit downmarket here. But with the new marina in operation Rick thinks that this part of town will soon be the smart place to live.'

'That's planning ahead with a vengeance! But I sure hope so—for your sake as much as his.'

Kerrie said quietly, 'Someone has got to start the trend. He thinks his *klinik* will be just the beginning.' She was quiet as they walked, thoughtful.

Working for Rick was one thing, but for Rick and Belle together? The whole thing was beginning to seem wrong. To leave honest Leon and work for conniving Belle Nader? Kerrie would have to be crazy, and she realised it now, in spite of the much higher salary that had been promised. Even that wasn't agreed yet.

They walked past the marina, where grizzled fishermen mended their nets, while at the smart end expensive yachts were being painted, or just washed down and the brass polished till it reflected the sun. Kerrie looked across at the Maharajah—and had a sudden shock. 'There it is—look, Kim. Gosh, how much better it looks with a coat of paint!' There was a scaffolding up at one end of the building, but at the other the walls gleamed white with new paint, and a gang of workmen busied themselves sawing and replacing timbers that had rotted. There was even a gardener, digging over the small patch of ground, and a barrow full of small shrubs stood by, waiting to be planted.

Kim said, 'I'm impressed. Rick certainly means business. I've never seen so many workmen on one house.'

Kerrie said, 'I knew he must have the determination. I wish I'd waited to see it until now. It really looks like the sort of place Madame Karela, Mr Singh or Madame Janar wouldn't mind coming to be treated, don't you think?'

'I suppose you're right.' The large barn-like doors had been replaced by louvred wood, painted white, and a portico had been added, with fluted pillars, to give a square of shade at the front. 'Can we see inside?' asked Kim.

Kerrie led the way. 'Let's see.' Inside the story was the same. The shutters at the windows had been painted green, and the sun streamed in. 'Can you see what it will be like when there's carpet here?' There was also a strong smell of some form of chemical, which they both realised was to get rid of the cockroaches and rats.

'Well, if it isn't Kerrie Snow! How nice to run into you again, Kerrie.' A tallish, stooped young man was coming out of the largest downstairs room with a clipboard and a sheaf of papers in his hand.

Kerrie turned in surprise at seeing her friend, the architect she had last met at the hospital in Kalang Bahru. 'Hello, Bob. What are you doing here?' Kerrie introduced the architect to Kim. 'Have you finished at Kalang, Bob?'

He shook Kim's hand politely, juggling his papers as he did so. 'This is a rush job. The client is offering the boys a bonus if they get it finished in four days.' He turned to Kim to explain, 'I'm getting a bit of a name for hospitals. These are mostly my men, but to please the client I've had to hire another ten.'

'Rick didn't seem to be in such a rush. I saw him at the beach this morning——'

'Who's Rick?' Bob looked puzzled.

'The owner—your client. Don't tell me you haven't even met Rick O'Grady?'

'My client isn't called Rick, I assure you.'

'But——' Kerrie felt a sense of caution, and didn't ask any more questions about the client. 'May we see the plans?'

Bob hesitated. 'Are you—a friend of the owner?'

Kerrie realised he didn't know of her connection with the Maharajah Klinik. 'I've been offered a job here.'

Bob stared. 'I didn't know you were leaving the Sultan.' He scratched his head. 'Oh, well, if you're part of the set-up, here, take a look.

Kerrie and Kim pored over the layout. 'Very impressive. You've done a great job—and so quickly too.'

Bob said, 'I'm just think of taking a break. Can I buy you ladies a cold drink?' He indicated the Chinese café over the road, with scrubbed wooden tables outside, and an appetising aroma coming from the kitchen windows. Seated at one of the tables, they ordered iced tea, and a plate of Nonya cakes, made of rice flour and shredded coconut. Bob took another sheet of paper from them to look at. 'This is the flat, Kerrie. It isn't finished yet, because the client wanted some alterations.'

'A new bathroom? How nice. The last one had a rat in it.' Kerrie spread the plans out. 'But Bob, this is a palace.'

'In keeping with the rest of the building, when I'm through with it.'

Kerrie's niggle of misgiving grew. Would this be so grand if it was for her? Rick must want it for himself. It would have been good manners to let her know. She began to think she had been rather thoughtlessly treated all round.

Kim said, 'I say, what's that being delivered now? It looks like a signboard.' They all looked across the road, where a flat piece of painted wood was handed down carefully from a truck. The truck drove away, and three workmen found two ladders. Two of them carefully carried the sign up and placed it over the pillared porch, while the man on the ground re-positioned them until he was satisfied.

Bob said, 'I'd better go and make sure they don't do anything wrong.' He rose. 'You'll excuse me?'

The girls remained at the wooden table, ordering ice-cream sodas while they watched. The sign was elegantly shaped, and there was already a delicate flowered border, round some rough letters the girls couldn't read. Once the screws were in, and all three men plus an anxious Bob were satisfied, they beck-oned another young man, who climbed up and placed a plank between the two ladders.

Kim said, 'He's the artist. He'll be painting the name of the *klinik*. This is very exciting, Kerrie. It's like seeing it in Fast Forward! An instant hospital. Can you see what he's painting? I love the curly letters—sort of Indian. Of course, silly me. The "Maharajah" would have to be in Indian-type letters.'

But Kerrie wasn't impressed. Her misgivings were growing by the second. She said without enthusiasm, 'Putting a great sign up there makes it look like an Indian take-away!'

The artist painted slowly and carefully. The girls lost interest, and talked of other things. When they looked again, the elaborate sign was finished, and the men were dismantling the platform and ladders. Above the classical portico was emblazoned, MAHARAJAH KLINIK, and underneath, in very clear smaller letters, 'Dr B. S. Nader'.

'She couldn't! I knew it! I just knew it!' Kim threw her hands in the air in disbelief.

'So Belle is the client! I bet Rick doesn't know anything about this. His name isn't even mentioned.' Kerrie felt sorry for him. He had sounded so very pleased with himself that morning.

'What do you think's going on?'

'I think, Kim, that Belle has pulled a fast one, as I might have suspected when I saw them together. She probably offered to hire the workmen—and, just in passing, gave them her own orders instead of what Rick wanted.'

'He won't stand for that, surely?'

Kerrie smiled. 'Well, I'm not sitting here indefinitely, just to see the expression on his face. In fact, I'm out of this project as from this moment. I want nothing whatever to do with this bad smell of a hospital. Come on, Kim, I want out.'

'Don't you feel a bit sorry for Rick? Sat upon by Leon, and now cheated out of his own hospital? Poor guy. I do. And here he is now.' Kim pointed. Rick O'Grady was striding jauntily along the street, his cotton jacket over one shoulder, and his head at a cheerful angle. He was alone, and had apparently had a most enjoyable day.

The girls watched as the good-looking young surgeon crossed the road and lifted his eyes ready to appreciate the changes that had been made to his wonderful new acquisition.

'Poor guy,' repeated Kerrie quietly, as his face changed, his shoulders lost their jaunty angle, and he turned away, before looking back at the signboard as though he couldn't believe his own eyes.

'Looks as though you're the only friend he's got, Kerrie. Do you think you ought to go over and commiserate?'

Kerrie shook her head. 'I—I can't, not now. Not after——' She didn't go on. Rick had crowed over her, spoken of her with something like scorn. Sorry as she was for an underdog, she knew she couldn't go and speak to Rick now. His words were still fresh in her mind. 'I'd been ready to work for him, Kim. Ready, as you know, to resign from the Sultan to work for him, knowing very well that it would be a struggle at the beginning until they got patients, and something of a reputation. Rick was willing to allow me to give up my job and my security. He played on my sympathy. It isn't going to happen again. Come on, Kim, it's time we went home.' Home to the Sultan. Home to apologise to Leon and acknowledge that he had been right not to give her her freedom to make an ass of herself.

Kim hesitated as Kerrie rose and went to the door, then reluctantly she followed. 'I guess it isn't too bad. He's still got a job here. The only trouble is that it isn't his *klinik*, but Belle's, so he isn't his own boss. He's just exchanged one chief for another.'

Rick was standing in the shadowy doorway, speaking earnestly to Bob, gesticulating towards the signboard. Kerrie turned away. 'He sounded so very pleased with himself this morning. I wonder how he'll get on with Belle Nader now? What sort of lovebirds will they be tonight?'

The two girls walked slowly away without looking back. Kim gave Kerrie's arm a squeeze. 'Don't let it prey on your mind, Kerrie. You're well out of it.'

'I could have made a bad mistake here, Kim. I've got a lot to thank Leon da Cruz for. And to think I accused him of—of slavery, when he wouldn't let me go!' They turned towards a cab rank. 'I wonder if he'll ever forgive me? Or want to?'

CHAPTER TEN

KERRIE and Kim almost didn't go to a movie that evening. They thought the drama at the Maharajah Klinik was much more real than a film. But when they saw that James Bond was on they agreed that they would like to see it. Though, as Kim said, 'It will probably be quite tame after what we witnessed today.'

'I should have gone to him.' Kerrie felt guilty. 'I stayed in the café with you and I should have gone to him.'

'You didn't owe him anything, remember?'

Kerrie nodded. 'I know. He probably went to find Belle and sort things out. But don't you see, Kim? It was Rick who asked me to join them. If Belle is in charge, I haven't had any dealings with her. I ought to straighten things out honourably with Rick.'

'Don't worry about that,' said Kim. 'Just come back to the Sultan. You know that even Sister Chan said she misses you. And I'm sure the professor does.'

'Why are you sure about him?'

Kim shrugged, but Kerrie continued to ask, and Kim said eventually, 'Kerrie, one night, some time ago, I wanted to talk to you. I wanted my anatomy book back. I went to your door several times, but there was no answer. Then next morning, very early,

I heard a noise, and I saw you creeping in with your shoes in your hand.'

There was a silence. Kerrie said, 'You knew where I'd been?'

'I guessed. The entire *klinik* was bursting with the drama of you and the prof saving that man's life. You don't have to be very good at maths to put two and two together.'

Kim's voice was very gentle, and Kerrie asked, 'So you think that was why I left?'

'I don't know. I just know that there was something more than a doctor-nurse relationship between you—and I thought it was marvellous. And then you just—said you had a blazing row and that you couldn't stay.'

Kerrie took a deep breath. 'Did anyone else see me?'

'I don't think so. Nobody has ever said anything.'

'Thank goodness.'

They had reached the cinema. Kim smiled. 'Come on, Kerrie, let's lee the movie! We can't do anything about Rick tonight.'

'All right.' They bought tickets, and waited a few moments while their eyes got used to the dark inside. Kerrie said, 'I do—you know—I'm very fond of Leon.'

'I know that too.'

Kerrie whispered, 'I should have confided in you. But everything happened so suddenly—Rick offering me the job, and Leon propos——'

Kim stopped suddenly, and Kerrie ran into her in the dark. 'He asked you to marry him?'

There was a chorus of 'Shh!' all round them, and

they found their seats and subsided to watch the film. Kerrie saw very little of it, as her mind went back to the relationship she had always had with Leon. It had always been special. He had singled her out at once, recognising her as the girl he had first met on the beach, wearing very little. . . But the proposal had been hurtful. He had been arrogant then, and patronising. And he had refused to explain how he was caught up in Rick's past. How could she possibly have accepted him on those terms?

When the girls came out into the sultry tropical night, jostled by others in a hurry to find a good dining place, Kim said, 'Come back to my place, Kerrie. We'll make Chinese tea and have a long talk.'

Kerrie agreed. 'I almost wish Sister Chan had put me on nights right away, instead of starting next Wednesday. It's been a long day.' She curled up on Kim's sofa, yawning, while Kim opened the take-away meal of *wanton mee* and fried rice, and put it on plates while she made tea.

'I'm on at six,' she said. 'But we'll have lunch together, OK?'

Kerrie left her to sleep, and went back to her own little flat, appreciating it so much more now. She was grateful to be here. In spite of her weariness, she felt alert suddenly, and she spent a long time at the window, looking out over the moonlit garden where the crickets sang as though trying to burst the sky.

She woke late, and wondered whether to go for breakfast. Hunger decided her, and she went along to the dining-room at ten. There was hardly anyone there, and she took coffee and a roll to her usual table. She almost wasn't part of this cosy, friendly place any more. But it was nice to be back, just for a while.

'Excuse me—may I join you? You are alone?'

'Yes, of course.' Kerrie's heart thumped. It was the good-looking secretary she had seen Leon with, smiling at. 'I'm Kerrie Snow. I've been on leave.'

'I've met Kim, but I don't know many people yet.' The girl was very softly spoken, and her English was perfect. She seemed to come from a good family. 'I knew who you were.'

'How did you know that?'

'Professor da Cruz told me about you helping him to save a man who was stabbed. He said you were extremely pretty, and you had blonde hair. You fit the description.' And the girl smiled, as she stirred her coffee. 'It must be a wonderful feeling to know you have saved a man's life.'

'Yes. Yes, it is.'

'And how do you like Malaysia, Kerrie?'

Kerrie smiled. 'It's home to me now. I don't really want to be anywhere else.' Yet she was at Leon's mercy now. Suppose he decided to release her from her contract? Would she really want to stay in Tajul as an employee of Belle Nader, which was the only other choice? It was a chilling thought. She asked the other girl where she came from, and they chatted about places they had visited. As she said her farewells, Kerrie watched her go, and knew she would make an ideal wife for Leon. She was jealous, of course, but it was impossible not to like her. Kerrie sighed very deeply, and swirled the remains of her coffee at the bottom of the cup. 'If this were tea, maybe there would be tea-leaves left, and I could tell my fortune.' She put the cup down and went outside to relax in the warmth and beauty of the garden.

When she heard footsteps on the walkway she slipped quickly into a grassy hollow by the lake, where she couldn't be seen from the hospital. It was warm and secret, and the herons and demoiselle cranes were incredibly lovely, their colours bright and clear in the morning sun, their movements graceful as they moved idly in the shallows, feeding, then stood like statues, basking as Kerrie was in the sun.

And then Leon da Cruz appeared on the top of a mound, standing outlined against the deep blue of the sky like a god, his figure again causing spontaneous admiration from a startled Kerrie. Yet he was unaware of himself, his face showing concern only for her. 'I thought it was you. Were you hoping I hadn't seen you?' He strode down the grassy hummock and sat beside her, his eyes searching her face. 'What happened?'

Kerrie felt wretched. 'I haven't been at the Morib very much. I came back here. Yesterday I was out with Kim most of the day. I'm so sorry, Leon. Was Reza trying to find me to take me to Kalang?'

'Yes. The Morib was the only address I had for you. They must have gone on without you when you weren't there.'

She said softly, 'You don't have to feel responsible for me, you know. I'll make out. The future is a little bit unclear at the moment, but if you don't mind me staying here just a little longer. . .? I love this garden very much. My life seems to be in your hands at the moment, and I feel I don't really deserve your good regard.'

He looked into her eyes, and then somehow his hand was tipping her face towards him. 'Stay as long as you like. You think for one minute I'd send you away?' And he kissed her on the lips. She didn't pull away, loving the warm feel of his mouth on hers. 'You look right in this garden, Kerrie. You look beautiful. I've tried to let go my recollections of you, but I can't.' He bent towards her and kissed her again, and this time the kiss lasted much longer. Her head began to feel light, as the pressure of his lips made magic in her senses, and made her lean towards him and put her hand on his smooth firm shoulder.

After a long time he drew away, but kept one arm around her shoulders. 'I have to go to KL in a few days; there's some business to attend to at the University. And after that——'

'You're off to Europe, I believe?'

'How did you——?' He smiled. 'News gets around!'

'Kim told me.'

'I really want this business with Rick settled before I go. As you know, I don't like the man, but if it's what you want—— Is this new *klinik* going to take long to get ready?'

Kerrie's heart felt empty at the idea of Leon's being miles away. But she had to accept that his life was no concern of hers, because she had rejected him. 'It's almost ready.' His hand was still on her shoulder, and unconsciously she leaned her cheek against its warmth. 'You won't have heard, though, that the name over the door is Dr B. S. Nader.'

Leon stiffened. 'Belle? In business with O'Grady? I suppose it's her way of getting back at me because I——'

'That could be something to do with it. She doesn't like you very much.'

'Yes.' His tone was grave. 'How did you know?'

'It doesn't matter.' Kerrie sat up straighter. 'Were you very close to her?'

'She seemed OK at the time, Kerrie. Not now.'

A nightingale trilled in the branch above them. The garden shimmered as the heat of the sun reached its maximum at noon. Kerrie wished time would stop at that moment, with them close together, and no need to face any more problems. Then Leon said, 'If Belle's name is up over the door, then she must have put in the money. I always suspected that the story of O'Grady's rich sheep-farming uncle giving him a loan was a lie.'

Kerrie said quietly, without meaning to hurt him, 'But then you always suspected Rick—all the time. You never had a good word for him, even when he worked quite adequately for you.'

'Maybe.' Leon's reply drifted over the lake like a memory, and she knew he was going to leave her. His hand loosened on her shoulder. But before he stood up, he leaned over and kissed her cheek softly, moving his lips against it as though never wanting to take them away.

She looked up as he stood. 'Good luck in Europe.'

'Will you come and see me before I leave?'

'If you really want me to.'

His smile didn't reach his eyes. 'Isn't that what friends do?'

She felt her eyes sting, and turned away before the salt sting turned into tears that he might see. 'I'll come.' Suddenly she didn't want him to leave her, and she turned round again with his name on her lips, forgetting the tears on her cheeks. But he had gone.

Kerrie clasped her arms round her knees and bent her head on them, shutting out the sleek blue-grey of the herons and the vermilion of the cranes. She knew why Leon had moved—she too could hear voices, as the nurses came off their shift at twelve-thirty. If they hadn't been disturbed, she wondered if she would have confessed how much she loved him. The knowledge, the admission, was trembling very near, ready to be acknowledged. But perhaps it was better that he never knew. He was too proud ever to repeat his offer of marriage. And his modest young secretary was beginning to be a part of his life. She would make him a sweet and loyal wife, a million times better for him than the beautiful but brash Belle Nader, who was at this very moment probably causing untold anguish to Rick O'Grady.

Kerrie sat up, her tears dry on her cheeks now. Rick was the reason she had almost left the Sultan— and Rick might very well need her now. Her conscience told her she should see him and make it clear that she wouldn't work for him. But she was reluctant even to see him again.

Kim came running across the garden, smiling. 'I

have some news for you! I've passed my last exams! Staff Nurse Mayang—how does it sound?'

'Kim, that's wonderful! I knew you would, but it's still great news. We'll celebrate as soon as——'

'As soon as you've sorted out your future! Go along, now, and put that pushy Dr Nader in her place. I know you can, Kerrie.'

'Or console Rick for taking the booby-prize? Who knows? Yes, it has to be done. I can't go on mooning around doing nothing. See you, Kim. And congratulations again.'

In a hurry now to get her affairs sorted out, Kerrie looked for a cab. But there was only a trishaw, which she hailed. The cyclist's sturdy legs pushed at the pedals, the muscles standing out with the constant exercise. Kerrie leaned back on the cushions and wondered what she would find when she reached the harbour.

The Maharajah Klinik gleamed pure white. Its shining imitation marble portico gave out grandly towards the pavement, with its own metal bridge over the monsoon drain in front. The gardens were packed with newly planted hibiscus bushes and ornamental plants, and the railings were painted a fresh dark green, to match the shutters. It was a transformation indeed. The name of Belle Nader still stood out, as the sole owner of the Klinik. Kerrie stood and stared, wondering what to do. The workmen seemed to have finished, and the building stood as though abandoned in its prime.

Kerrie crossed the road. Then she saw that the front doors were ajar and there was someone in the shadowy foyer. Probably a watchman. She pushed a door further open, and went in. '*Salaam*. Is anyone here?' she called.

The man at the shiny new desk beside a rubber plant unwound himself from his chair. By his height she guessed who it was before he opened a shutter to give more light. 'Hello, Bob. What a marvellous achievement! I wouldn't have recognised this place. I hope everyone got their bonus.'

Bob shook his head and smiled. 'They did. But what a situation to be in! I took my orders from Dr Nader—and now I find that the legal owner is a Mr O'Grady.'

'So what happens now?'

'Damned if I know, Kerrie. One person owns it—but another person has paid for all the improvements. I'm glad I'm not a lawyer.'

Kerrie said, 'Do you know where I can find either of these persons? I want to know which of them thinks he's employing me.'

'Don't know, I'm afraid. But the janitor will be back on duty in a few minutes—I'm just filling in for him. He might know.'

'May I take a look at the other rooms?'

'Sure, go ahead. I'd better stay here, in case of thieves. Dr Nader would have my head. What a difference, Kerrie, between working here and working at the Kalang. There's nothing but bitterness and commercialism here.'

She agreed wholeheartedly. 'The atmosphere in Kalang was like that of a family. I know Leon moaned about the low level of efficiency, but I know which hospital I'd prefer to work in.'

There was the sound of the doors being thrust

open, and Belle's voice cut through the dimness of the interior. 'And where is that, Kerrie?'

'What?' Kerrie tried to stall her by not understanding the question.

'Which hospital would you prefer to work in?' Belle was wearing European costume today— another of her perfectly tailored silk suits, which showed off her superb figure without being too immodest.

Kerrie tried to be humorous. 'The one that pays me at the moment.'

'But you prefer the Sultan, no doubt—the one with the handsome proprietor.' Belle's voice was dripping with sarcasm. She walked further into the room and greeted Bob. 'Good afternoon. Where's the janitor?'

'I let him go for some lunch, Doctor.'

'Lunch? It's almost tea time.' She turned to Kerrie. 'Actually, I'm glad you're here. We must have a meeting to decide on the minimum staffing levels. I've engaged this chap to be doorkeeper, but I don't think we'll keep him, not if he takes three-hour lunch breaks. When will be convenient for you?'

'I'm free now.'

'Good. Then we can go up to the flat and get down to business.' And she led the way to a door at the side of the staircase, and pressed a button. The door slid back to reveal a lift. 'Come on, Kerrie.' They glided upwards, and the lift opened automatically in the upstairs flat.

Kerrie tried not to exclaim. This was very definitely Belle's apartment. It was decorated throughout in soft pastel shades, with occasionsal splashes of vivid colour in pictures, cushions and lampshades.

Belle led the way purposefully. 'This is my office. I haven't got all the shelving I need yet, but the safe is installed, and I have all the relevant documentation on disk, so sit down here, and we'll go over the staff and the salaries, and make an estimate of our runnings costs.' She beckoned Kerrie to sit opposite a computer screen, and switched it on. After a moment or two the name of the *klinik* flashed on to the screen; then Belle's name with the title 'Director' beside it.

Kerrie watched as the names popped on the screen one after another. 'Director of Medicine, Dr B. S. Nader. Director of Surgery, Mr R. N. O'Grady.' She said, 'So that's where Rick has ended up.'

Belle smiled her crocodile smile. 'Rick has done me a very great favour. I was desperate to do something really big to get my own back on Leon da Cruz.'

'But why?'

'Oh, don't tell me you don't know! We were almost engaged, remember? I had the chance of a half-share in his entire empire. My career was going to take off with a bang when he suddenly told me that we could be no more to each other than good friends. Good friends!' As Belle spat out the words, Kerrie felt sick at the way marriage to Leon was to Belle simply a business opportunity. Belle saw Leon as a string of profitable enterprises. There was never a word about love. 'Oh, yes, I did think of suing him for breach of promise, but that would have made me look petty in the newspapers. This is a much better way. Start up in competition! A big advertising campaign, proving that the Sultan overcharges; and a small staff, so that our overheads aren't too high at first. Oh, yes, Kerrie Snow, revenge is very sweet.'

'But why take it out on Rick? He's a nice guy.'

Belle looked at her pityingly. 'You mean you went blindly into this Maharajah business with Rick without knowing his past history? He is a declared bankrupt, you innocent child. No bank would ever lend him a dime.'

Kerrie was silent for a moment. 'Is that what Leon has against him?'

'I don't know all the details. They knew one another many years ago—I think the families were friends. But I know that Rick has no money except what Leon pays him, and he had to coax some wealthy distant cousin to finance this venture.'

'And what happened to that money?'

'The cousin backed out. The money for this place was raised by me. I'm not a millionairess, but I have a good name and several rich friends. The Maharajah is my hospital now, and Rick O'Grady is employed by me to help get my own back on Leon da Cruz. I take it you're also interested in a little revenge? He refused to release you from your contract, didn't he? There's no need to worry. With me in charge, we'll soon be making inroads into his clientele. Rick couldn't do it, Kerrie. He's a simple soul—no business drive. No, he'll soon thank me for taking over. You too. Your job is a responsible one. You'll both do all right with me.'

CHAPTER ELEVEN

KERRIE took a cab to the Sultan Ali Tabatabai Klinik, her head in a daze. She called in at the nurses' apartments, but Kim had gone shopping, and left a note that she would be back about six. Kerrie took a shower and changed into a fresh dress. She wanted to talk to someone, but Kim wasn't around. Leon might be in, but she felt shy of just calling. She sat for a while close to the telephone, trying to pluck up the courage to ring him, and wishing Kim would come home early. But at last she realised that Leon da Cruz was the only person to speak to. It was only right that he knew what was being planned. She put the phone down without ringing and walked across the grass to his apartment.

She rang the bell. There was a light inside, so someone must be home. After a moment, the door was opened by the pretty secretary. Kerrie stumbled over her words, embarrassed and distressed to find her here. 'I—sorry—I'll come back later.'

Leon appeared behind the girl. 'Kerrie, come on in,' he invited.

The girl said, 'Please do. I'm just leaving.' She picked up a folder of papers. 'Just catching up on some work,' she said rather pointedly. Kerrie felt wretched.

Leon recognised her distress. He put his hand

gently on her elbow and led her in. 'Sit down. There's something wrong. Can I get you a drink?'

'I'm disturbing you.'

'No, no—we'd finished. Silvi was just telling me about her family in Sabah. It wasn't important. We've finished preparing the papers I'm taking to Kuala Lumpur.'

Kerrie sat for a moment, trying to work out her thoughts. 'I feel as though it's I who's betraying you. In my anxiety to get away, I forgot to tell her that I'm having nothing to do with it. Hand in my resignation. I won't work for her.'

Leon went away, and came back with a glass of his favourite white wine. 'Here. Now, start at the beginning, Kerrie. There's no hurry. Is it about O'Grady?'

'In a way. Did you know he was a bankrupt?'

'Yes, of course I knew.'

She didn't look at Leon as she went on. 'Is that why you don't like him?'

'No, that isn't the reason. I told you, I've sworn not to talk about that to anyone.'

'But you knew that he couldn't get a loan from anyone except a relative?'

'Yes. Yes, I was aware that he couldn't fulfil his silly threat of setting up against me unless he had money from his family. And, knowing his family, I doubted that source.'

Kerrie moaned in the agony of having to go through all the venom and bitter greed for possessions that Belle Nader had poured out in her cruel triumph. 'But Belle is financing him.'

'I gathered that.'

'I didn't realise. I'm supposed to be helping her.'

Leon said quietly, 'Well, she would assume, as you turned me down and wanted to resign from the Sultan, that you share her dislike of me.'

'Leon, I feel it's all my fault. You broke off the affair with Belle, and she hated that. If you hadn't done that, there'd be no Maharajah. Rick would have had to pull out of the whole thing. As it is, Belle saw her chance of opening in competition, and spreading false rumours about your business practices. She's a fiend, Leon—an evil woman, with no conscience or decent feelings at all.'

Leon sat beside her and took her hand in his. He said gently, 'So don't you think it was right for me to break with her anyway? I didn't love her. You wouldn't have wanted me to be tied for life to a woman like that, would you?'

'If you had loved her, she would have treated you loyally, I'm sure. Maybe she didn't love you, but she knew her financial prosperity was linked with your success. She would have put all her energies into making the Sultan a success, instead of trying to ruin it.'

He stood up then, and strode across the room and back, frowning with concentration. 'The fact remains that I don't love her, never did, and made it clear when I realised she was beginning to treat me as if I were her fiancé—when she bought herself that diamond, for instance. Then I scented danger, and made the break as clean and as civilised as I could. I'm so very relieved that I discovered her true nature. I only ever admired her for her beauty and her efficiency. And now I don't fear her, Kerrie. She hasn't got the breadth of vision to make a success in a caring profession. And you see, I couldn't feel the same about her after I met you.' He stopped walking and stood in front of her, looking down. 'You showed me something I hadn't experienced before. In you I met for the first time a woman who could be beautiful, gentle and generous—and yet have a firm spirit and a strong sense of morality and duty that I felt matched my own.'

Completely lost for words now, Kerrie could only say, 'No—no.'

'That's how I felt. And I compared Belle to you, Kerrie, and she came out a very poor and tarnished second. So it was right that I'd apologised when I did for wasting her time, and suggested that she wouldn't find happiness tied to me, and that I certainly wasn't even considering marriage.'

Kerrie swallowed. 'Are you really not afraid of this plot? She intends to pay her staff very little at first—pay them with promises, if you like. She thinks she can break even in six months.'

Leon chuckled. 'Don't forget, my dear, that Belle doesn't know you've come straight to me with all her wicked plots and conspiracies. She would never have imagined that, would she?'

'No, I guess she wouldn't. I ought to have told her what she could do with her job. But I was in too much of a hurry to get away from her influence. She knows how to manipulate people, you see.'

'But not you, Kerrie. Never you.' He paused, and said 'Would it make it any easier if I asked you to start work again right away?'

Staring hard at the floor, Kerrie said, 'I couldn't.

I want to, but it wouldn't be right. I walked out on you. I left because I felt I ought to be loyal to Rick. Belle Nader has no hold on me like that. But I still owe Rick something. All right, he isn't a very good manager of money, but that doesn't make him a criminal.'

'No, I suppose it doesn't. But he's still not an honourable man, and I'll always find it impossible to admire him. Don't you even feel jealous at his affair with Belle? He was falling for you until he met someone with more money. That's typical of the man, you know.'

Kerrie stood up then. 'If only you wouldn't keep making cruel remarks about him, Leon! I must go. I feel wretched. I want to talk things out with Rick, but I think my duty now is to go and tell Belle that I'm resigning. I should have done it before. Good-night, Leon—I'm glad things aren't going to be as bad for you as Belle was threatening.'

'Why do you feel wretched?'

She was already at the door. Turning, she looked into his eyes, and told him the truth. 'Because you could be so perfect. Yet you keep on showing me your own streak of—of cruelty, and it—it—spoils everything!' She was through the door in seconds, and had closed it firmly behind her. Than she ran.

Kim was home. 'You've been to see the professor?'

'Yes.' The professor. . . Kerrie's own dear, secret love, whom she loved so much, yet who disappointed her so much. 'You weren't here, and I had to tell someone what a wicked witch I found myself working for.'

'Belle Nader isn't a nice woman—everyone knows that.'

'If only I could find out what Rick thinks of it all!'

Kim said, 'Give him a call. He has to be home some time.'

Kerrie dialled. After a long time, his cleaning lady answered. Kerrie said, 'If you see him, tell him Kerrie is at the Sultan.'

Kim said as Kerrie put the phone down, 'What did she say?'

'Not a lot. I don't think she understands English. Well? Shall I take you out for dinner? We must celebrate your exams.'

Kim shook her head. 'How about we make an instant party? Invite all the girls, and have it in the dining-room?'

'Great idea. Let's go and see the manageress. Any men invited?'

'Everyone can bring someone. How's that?'

'Good idea. I'll nip out and buy some drinks. Anything else while I'm going? What records can we get together?'

'Kerrie Snow, you aren't allowed to buy anything—it's my party! Here, take this.' Kim gave Kerrie some dollar bills. 'I'll organise the music and some food while you're gone.'

Glad to have her mind taken off her uncertain future, Kerrie hurried to the nearest shop and bought a cardboard box full of assorted chilled canned drinks. She tried to put Belle Nader out of her mind. Much as she wanted to ring and resign from the Maharajah, she felt it was only right to consult Rick O'Grady first. What did she know about him? He was a bankrupt. He was a woman-iser. His charm on their first date had been all an act, a carefully worked out plan to make her trust him. His opinion of her as 'frigid' was unfair. . . True, Philip Wentworth had thought the same, but Kerrie knew that her feelings were as passionate as any normal woman's when roused by the right man. Philip had dropped her too—yet in a way he had done her a favour, showing her that she just hadn't met the right man. Mr Right—was there such a man for Kerrie Snow, or would she never again meet a man like Leon da Cruz, who could carry her to the heights of satisfied desire, of glorious and complete fulfilment?

Some couples were already dancing when Kerrie got back, and she made herself useful with the plastic cups, mixing a skilful punch with white wine and orange juice, ginger ale and chopped fruits. Jami Arul came over to help. 'You should have been a surgeon, Kerrie.'

She looked up, delighted to see him. 'Hi, Jami. Why a surgeon?'

'The way you chopped up that starfruit—a real cutter, you are!'

'Don't you mean I ought to be working in a Chinese restaurant, chopping ginger?'

He smiled. 'It's good to see you, Kerrie. Come and dance with me.' As they danced to the rhythms of the latest Singapore rock star, he went on, 'You never did take any notice of my warning about Rick O'Grady, did you?'

She smiled, cynical now, 'Jami, there was no need. He found a richer, more willing lady.'

Jami stopped dancing for a moment, losing his step. 'So why in the name of heaven did you want to leave the Sultan? It doesn't make sense. I thought you left because you had to stick up for this dude. If he left you, what's the hassle?'

Kerrie laughed, as the music swelled. 'Enjoy yourself, Jami. I'll tell you the answer to that one when I know it!'

But, as the party grew noisier, Kerrie began to think out what Jami had said. Rick, and Rick's honour, had been the reason she left the Sultan. Yet he hadn't proved very honourable himself—nor very caring towards Kerrie's feelings. Was it really a matter of principle? Or had Kerrie used Rick as an excuse for refusing to marry Leon, because she thought Leon had only proposed as a matter of duty? With feelings even more mixed up than usual, Kerrie left the crowded dining-room and sought her favourite resting place, in the grassy hollow beside the lake. The music throbbed faintly in the background, and she rested beside her favourite tree-trunk. The crickets chirped in unison, wave after wave of shrill sound that by its very repetition was soon ignored.

Her thoughts then were only memories. She couldn't stop thinking of all the compliments Leon had paid her. 'Generous—beautiful—with the depth of morality and duty—firmness—spirit. . .' Oh, Leon, Leon, my only love! Too much firmness. Too much spirit. He might have known how easily I could have been swayed by his physical power—yet he refused to pressure me. He wanted me to come to him freely. And I turned him down. . .

There was a rustle of branches, as someone came towards her, and she jumped up, not wishing to be thought anti-social at Kim's party. Rick's voice came darkly through the trees. 'I came to the party but I don't know if I'm welcome. Kim said you'd be here.'

Kerrie sank down again with her back against her tree. Rick stood for a moment, then he too sank down, and sat cross-legged beside her. Kerrie said, 'I suppose I should be glad we've managed to meet.'

'It has been a bit of a hide-and-seek. I thought you did it on purpose, to show me what a heel I've been. Can I say I don't blame you?'

Kerrie's natural goodwill spoke out. 'Don't speak like that, Rick. All I want to know is what you feel about the way things are turning out.'

'That's all?'

'Yes, that's all.'

'And if I say everything's hunky-dory, then you're satisfied?'

'Not satisfied, Rick, but I didn't want to get out completely until I knew it was what you would have wanted.'

'Kerrie, you're a brick!'

'Go on. Tell me how it all happened?'

But there was a long silence, and Kerrie realised suddenly that Rick was crying. It upset her. He wasn't the type to give in to emotion. Yet he had once said that there was more inside him than she knew. A 'nine-stone weakling', had been Rick's account of himself. After a while, he tried to speak, but he was sadly, frighteningly distressed. She had never imagined he could be like this. She reached out and took his hand, and he gripped it with both his. 'I don't think anyone has ever stood up for me the way you have,' he said quietly.

She waited, but as he didn't speak, she said, 'You didn't plan for Belle Nader to take over your hospital?'

'Never. She was sweet as pie. Fluttering eyelashes, tears—the lot. Da Cruz had dumped her, could I give her a job!' There was a long pause. He went on with a sniff, his voice stronger, 'A willing victim. I've no excuse, Kerrie. I'm just an archetypal idiot.'

'I didn't tell her I wanted nothing to do with the Maharajah if she's in charge, but I want to resign, and I waited to ask you if it was OK.'

'Go ahead, love. The sooner the better.'

'Are you getting out?'

'I can't. The only money I ever had is in there. Now that the Malaysian authorities have my details, I won't be able to work anywhere else. She's got me by the short and curlies.'

'And if your Maharajah doesn't succeed? Leon isn't a bit worried by her challenge.'

'I can see that. He wasn't born yesterday. He has Belle's measure, just as he has mine.' Kerrie was touched by the sound of sincerity in Rick's voice. He went on, 'I only hope you haven't been ruined by being associated with us.'

'I don't think I can stay here now.'

'Why on earth?'

'Principle, I suppose. I—called Leon a lot of names because of the way he was treating you.'

Again there was a silence between them, and Rick suddenly put his head in both hands. 'He didn't tell you why we hated each other?'

'No. He said he'd promised not to.'

Rick said without lifting his head, 'You didn't suspect anything?'

She looked uncomfortable at his bent head. 'I'm probably very naïve, Rick. I just—didn't like the way he spoke to you. I thought he was being unfair.'

Rick suddenly unpleated himself and stood up like a miraculous untying of the Gordian knot. He stood straight, lifting his head. His hair reflected the golden moonlight. 'Kerrie, I'm grateful to you for your trust. I apologise to you for the great wrong I did you. I'm going to tell you something now that I've never told anyone. I know you'll respect the confidence of a con-man who doesn't even deserve forgiveness.'

She looked up at him. She recalled all the points against him that she had thought up that night. 'I think you're going to tell me why.'

'What else can I do? No one has ever given me that much trust. Kerrie, you'll never speak to me again, but I have to tell you. Back home, Leon was a young surgeon, and I was a sheep-farmer.'

'In Australia?'

'Sure—Queensland. He never told you?'

'No.'

Rick drew in a troubled breath. 'Our families were close. Anyway, his father helped me through medical school. I guess Leon was like an older brother to me, in a way. After I graduated, instead of asking me to pay back my tuition fees, da Cruz's father lent me another half-million bucks to start a country clinic—nursing and convalescent. It could have been a winner—except that having money went to my head, and I expanded the place into a health farm without proper advice. The whole thing collapsed. I couldn't ever pay back what I owed his family.'

'So you never repaid the money?'

'I had nothing to give him when his own business went into liquidation—only because he had no collateral. He was relying on my being a success.'

'That's sad.'

Rick said bitterly, 'Sadder. Leon's father died— they said it was from shame. They'd quarrelled over me. And he died before Leon and he could make things up.'

Kerrie said softly, 'Thanks for telling me all this.'

'I felt bad, naturally. And as a bankrupt I couldn't start out again on my own. Even though indirectly it was my fault that things went bad in Queensland, Leon still felt it was his duty to help me out. He took me on at the Sultan, on condition I didn't try and take on any other ventures. Said he'd give me a job until I could build up some savings. I guess I just hated being a poor relation.'

Kerrie took a deep breath. Only now did she understand fully the enmity between the two men— Rick's resentment at being a receiver of charity; Leon's sadness that his father died as a result of Rick's foolishness. She said sadly, 'You did give a very good impression of a confident young surgeon, you know—bursting with ambition and ideas. It was easy to believe that Leon envied you your independence and drive, and genuinely feared your competition.'

Rick nodded in the darkness. 'The biter bit. Conman taken for a ride. Whatever way you say it,

Kerrie, you can't help feeling secretly pleased that I've got my come-uppance from Belle Nader. She won't even sleep with me now, unless she's desperate. It's a hair-shirt and grovelling for a crust for the next few years for yours truly.'

Kerrie tried to think of the right words. 'I had to know, Rick. I'm grateful because you told me everything. I know what to do now.'

'Honey, you were the first to stand by me, after Leon. It wasn't an easy feeling to cope with, having someone standing by me—standing up for me. Especially against Leon da Cruz. He was always being held up to me as an example of what I could be if I chose. You had to be one very special lady, to stick by me in the face of Leon's disapproval. That's why I've told you everything—and why I trust you to keep it to yourself.'

'Sure. I won't say anything.'

'I saw the way you were with Leon. Is it on or off?'

'Completely off.' And she wept inwardly at Leon's obstinacy in keeping the sorry tale to himself. If he had explained it all, she wouldn't have been so quick to take Rick's side. Yet she felt a deep admiration at Leon's ability to keep his promise to someone who clearly wasn't capable of keeping any promise to anyone; and she felt a small bubble of pride, because Leon had said that her sense of duty was the same as his.

The music surged from the nurses' home, as someone opened the windows. Rick held out his hand. 'Bye, Kerrie. Be happy. You're some sheila!'

'Happy? Me?'

Rick hung his head. 'I didn't mean any harm to you, you know. If I could do something to help, I would.'

'It doesn't matter. Something will turn up, I suppose. I might even apply for a permanent job at Kalang. I'd miss Kim, but they're nice people out there, and I could pretend I was happy.'

Just then they heard the siren of an ambulance, and tyres screeched as it drew up at the door of the *klinik*. Kerrie ran across the grass to see if she could be any help. Three stretchers were carried out, met by the houseman in Casualty. Hurried instructions were passed from doctor to staff. 'Road accident! Crush injuries. We'll need all theatres.'

Kerrie went up to Theatre. 'Can you use me?'

'Glad to have you.' The surgeon on call was already scrubbing up. 'Thanks, Kerrie. Can you phone down and see who can take Theatre Three?'

She rang. Leon da Cruz answered. 'I'll be there in two minutes. Is it Kerrie?'

'Yes.'

'I'm glad.'

For the next hours three surgeons toiled to rebuild shattered bodies. There was no time to look around at the other members of the team. But when the patients were safely in Recovery, drips in position, and monitors making the right noises, Kerrie heard Leon's voice, quiet but appreciative. 'It was good of you to give us a hand, Rick.'

'About time I did something human. Hope they make it.' And Rick was gone, waiting for no thanks.

CHAPTER TWELVE

KERRIE set out by cab to the Maharajah Klinik, to face Belle Nader and hand in her resignation. It was almost noon. The gardener was hoeing between the hibiscus bushes, and picking up the dead leaves. The uniformed janitor stood proudly at the entrance, smiling toothlessly at passers-by, in case they were prospective clients.

Kerrie went in. She was unhappy to be leaving Tajul, but her heart was strong, now that she knew at last what she had to do. There was a masculine-looking Chinese lady at the desk, her eyebrows plucked almost away, and her mouth plastered with crimson lipstick. 'Good day to you,' she said.

'*Salaam*. I'm Kerrie Snow. Is it OK to go up and have a word with Dr Nader?'

'Ah—yes, Miss Snow. I will ring up. Please to wait.'

While the receptionist buzzed the flat, Kerrie looked around the foyer. Belle had put up pictures—scenes of Malaysian life, and a couple of rather good water colours of Singapore's waterfront. There was no doubt she had the knowhow to make a go of this place. Yet Leon hadn't been troubled. Only time would tell who was right.

Kerrie was directed to the lift. As she stepped out at the flat, Belle was waiting, a vision in a green and yellow chiffon Malay suit, with her hair swept up in a white chiffon turban. 'Good day, Kerrie. Have you given any thought to the ideas I gave you yesterday?'

Kerrie opened the briefcase in her hand, and, walking to the desk, she tipped its contents out, so that the papers piled up, and some fell on the floor. 'Quite a lot of thought. They're all yours, Dr Nader. And my resignation.'

Belle's voice hardened, as she looked at the untidy mess Kerrie had made of the office. 'Did O'Grady tell you say that?'

'No, he certainly did not. I don't take advice, Dr Nader. I make up my own mind. I'm sometimes wrong—very wrong, but in this case, I know I'm right. I was interested to take on the job of Administrator when it was just a case of starting up a new enterprise. But I don't want to have any part in a case of calculated revenge—it isn't my scene. Goodbye.'

'Wait! If it's a case of working for me instead of Rick, I guarantee he has a big say in what goes on here. I put myself in charge only to help him, Kerrie, can't you see that? He needs strong leadership— which I can give him. Think again?'

'Why should I? I've said what I came to say.'

'Don't you need the job?'

Kerrie looked at the beautiful face across the desk, and despised her. 'I hope I'm never so hard up that I need to work for you, Belle.'

'You're not going back to the Sultan? Surely not?'

'No. At least you have that satisfaction. My life is nothing to do with you from now on. I just think that what you plan to do is despicable.'

Belle said, her tone conciliatory, 'Maybe you

think I've been—a trifle harsh with Rick. I didn't mean it to look like that. I just wanted to give him a helping hand. He isn't much of a businessman, poor darling.'

'And even less when you get your hands on him!'

Belle took a deep beath. 'We're—sorry to lose you, Kerrie. I have to say your reputation is very good.'

Kerrie almost laughed. 'Maybe I should tell you that I was down at the beach one morning, and I heard you and Rick talking about me. I heard what you both really thought of me, Belle. I think you thought you could manipulate me by flattery or something. I believe you thought that just because I'm idealistic I lack common sense too. Sorry, Belle—I do know what's going on. I may have been naïve when I first came to Malaysia, but getting to know you has educated me in lots of ways.'

'Damn! I was counting on you. I'll double your salary. A share of the profits?'

'I'm glad you're grovelling, Belle, because it gives me a great sense of satisfaction to say what I'm going to now. People like you believe that everyone has a price. I don't. I won't be bought. Goodbye, Belle. I can't say I wish you luck.' Kerrie didn't wait for the fancy lift, but went to the door, slammed it behind her, and ran down the staircase and out into the street.

After she had got her breath back, Kerrie began to be quite pleased with the way she handled that. She walked slowly into town, knowing that the next call she had to make was not going to be so straightforward, because she was dreadfully and completely in love with the person she had to see.

Leon was in his apartment. 'Kerrie! How nice of you to come back. I was just going to do a ward-round. Come on in. Will you come to the ward with me? I'd like to think you were still part of the Sultan, you know.'

She saw from his face that there was no blame of her in him, in spite of the hurtful words she had said to him—words that she now knew were unjustified. She said rather breathlessly, 'I won't stay a moment. I had to come while what I have to say was still burning in my head.'

'OK, go on.' His expression was attentive. 'If you can wait till six, we could discuss it over drinks.'

'No, we couldn't.' Kerrie refused to sit down. 'Let me just talk—please?'

'Sure.'

'I have a very abject apology to make, and I want to make it now, totally and honesty. I'm heartily sorry for doubting you and your intentions towards Rick O'Grady. I've never been so wrong about anything, and I'm so sorry.'

'But wait——'

'I can't wait. I have to say it, Leon. Rick told me everything.'

'Rick did? He actually confessed the whole thing? What happened in Australia? What he did?'

'Yes,' said Kerrie. 'He said I had a right to know. In fact, he was very upset.'

Leon whistled. 'He has a conscience!'

Kerrie nodded. 'And so have I. I've been so wrong about you. I've got things straight now, and I'll always be ashamed of the way I spoke to you. I—want to say thank you for always being decent and kind, in spite of my bad manners. I wish you every good fortune in the future, and I hope you'll accept my apology.'

He came towards her, hands out. 'Kerrie, Kerrie, you don't owe me an apology. I would have told you if I hadn't promised. . . But thank you for saying it. I'm glad I don't have to keep secrets from you any more, darling.'

She backed away. 'And I think your new girl— Silvi—would be very good for you; much less of a pain in the neck than I was. Goodbye, Leon. I never really enjoyed my work—my life—so much as when I was here.' And with tears streaming down her cheeks, she ran out of his door, hating herself for giving way, but very relieved that she had delivered her apology, and that he had forgiven her.

It was a very restrained and calm Kerrie who went to dinner at the Morib that evening. 'Has my friend Kim arrived yet for my farewell meal?' she asked.

'Kim, dear?' Madame Janar was dressed in a long shimmery robe with a matching drape round her head. She seemed abstracted. 'I have an old friend come to wish you well.'

Kerrie turned, to see Madame Karela, a vision of efficiency and chic in a grey silk dress draped round her slim figure, high-heeled shoes, and with her abundant blue-rinsed hair in a coil on top of her head. Kerrie's self-control let her down, as she ran to embrace the old lady. 'Oh, when I think of how you used to look, *madame*—how we used to sit and chat! It does make me happy to see you so well.'

Madame Karela retorted, with suspiciously bright eyes, 'You thought the old hag was finished, didn't you, my dear? But you pulled me through. You talked to me about what young living was all about— and suddenly I wasn't willing to let it all go. You saved my life, just as much as you saved young Kamal's here.' Kamal had appeared from some recess in the hotel lobby, and stood beside his mother, the only sign of his ordeal being a long faded scar under his ear.

Madame Janar said, 'Now, Kerrie, if you can bear sharing your dinner with half the local Chamber of Commerce, I've arranged for your meal to be served in my private apartment.'

'But why?'

An attentive Malay butler opened the door for them, and the four of them, including Kamal, walked through into the private apartment. 'Hi, Kerrie!'

'Kim, why are you in here before us? What's going on?'

'Sit down, and I'll explain.' Kerrie obeyed. The butler came round with a tray of orange juice and champagne. Kim was laughing. 'You told me about the threat from the Maharajah and its charming new proprietor, Kerrie, and I told Madame Janar. We decided to do something about it. These people are only a few of many grateful patients of the Sultan who want to make sure that no bad publicity is allowed to be published against it. So this is a private meeting to decide what tactics we take if and when Belle Nader starts spreading false rumours. I wanted to do something—we all did. Want to help?'

'You know I do if I can.'

'Good. Then as soon as our guest arrives we can

start our working dinner, with Madame Janar in the chair.'

Kerrie was smiling. 'So businesslike! What a marvellous idea. Good for you, Kim. What guest are we waiting for?'

'Only Leon. He said he wouldn't be long.'

Kerrie felt as though she had been winded by a heavy object. Seeing Leon again when she thought she had made her graceful farewell. . . 'I suppose—it's only sensible for him to know what's going on.'

'Particularly as he'll be going to Europe soon, and can't keep an eye on the campaign himself.'

Kerrie agreed, faintly. She at least had time to compose herself, so that when Leon da Cruz walked in, superbly handsome in a white tuxedo and black tie, she was able to shake his hand, along with all the others, and maintain a dignified smile.

Madame Karela led the meeting, though the splendid meal of lobster, followed by chicken à la Morib, and a host of desserts, tended to make the conversation a round of appreciative remarks and compliments to the chef. Kerrie was particularly pleased to be seated between Kamal Janar and Kim, so that it wasn't necessary to exchange more than a casual word or two with Leon.

'So we are decided,' Madame Karela was making notes, 'that if any attack whatsoever is mounted against our beloved Sultan, a series of advertisments go out, genuine testimonials from patients who have benefited from the superb treatment we have gained from there, giving a simple appreciation of the quality of surgery, medicine and nursing care. I have at least seventeen ex-patients so far who would be happy to put their names to such testimonials.'

Leon ventured, 'You think this is essential?'

Madame Karela smiled indulgently at him over her coffee cup. 'No. I'm sure they would not dare to try to defame you. Half of Tajul—in fact of the entire state—knows your reputation, Leon. It would be sheer madness to try to pretend their treatment hasn't been of the very best. But, being crazy, Nader might try—and she might probably undercut your rates. You must agree that a swift campaign on these lines is easier and less bloody than a lawsuit.'

'I have to agree with you there.'

Madame Karela stood up. 'Ladies and gentlemen, I must be off, I'm afraid. I'm late for a meeting of the Chamber of Commerce.'

It only took seconds for the Janars, and for Kim to make equally valid excuses. Suddenly the room was empty, but for Kerrie and Leon. He looked across the table and smiled broadly, his eyes twinkling as they had on that very first meeting on Tajul beach. 'Oh, dear, now we must make boring conversation with each other, until one of us manages to make an excuse to leave.'

She looked across the table at him, and loved him. 'I didn't think I'd see you again.'

Their looks intermingled. He murmured, 'I have an idea. Maybe we should go to my place and talk?'

She looked away. 'Do you really——'

'I've loved you far too long to be willing to wait any longer.' He reached across the table, between coffee-cups and screwed-up napkins, and caught her hand. 'Can you think of a single reason why not? Am I still arrogant and patronising?'

'No.' With a heart beginning to fill with joy, she said, 'You never were, Leon. Never. You were only honest. I know that now.'

He was round the table in a moment, holding her close, and she melted against him, suddenly gloriously happy. He stroked her hair, and kissed her forehead. 'What friends we have, Kerrie—to go to such lengths to make sure you don't escape me again.'

From the depths of his embrace, she whispered, 'You can't imagine what a jealous woman I can be. Any female who looks at you with fluttering eyelashes—or who brings you a gift in gratitude for curing her illness; they will all be my enemies.'

He looked down at her. 'You couldn't make enemies—it isn't in your nature. Let's go home, my jealous darling! If I imagined for a moment you were speaking the truth——'

She stopped his talk with a kiss. Somehow they found his Pontiac in the Morib car park, and made their way back to the Sultan. As soon as the door was closed behind them, their longing surfaced with a wild abandon, and he carried her to the bed, making her his own, and loving her until she begged for more.

It was far into the night when they woke and made love again, enchanted and besotted with each other. 'The moon is beautiful,' Kerrie whispered. 'Almost as beautiful as you. Let's walk in the garden?'

He pulled on his shirt and trousers, and Kerrie put her dress on over her naked body, and they walked with bare feet across the grass. Leon whispered, 'I hope none of the patients is looking out of a window.'

'We'll go to my "alone" place, where we can't be seen—and then it won't ever be a sad place again.'

'Has it been terribly sad, Kerrie? Poor child, so many miles from home.'

'The Sultan is home. It was home almost as soon as I arrived here. It wasn't being far from England that made it sad. It was just that—I was separated from you. I was stupid. I should always have believed you.'

He murmured, his lips against her hair, 'It isn't always easy to recognise who to believe.'

'I desired you from the moment I saw you. But that isn't love, is it?'

'Maybe it is. I felt exactly the same. You've no idea how exhilarated I felt when I walked into the ward and found you—my sea-maiden. I knew I wanted you then. Every time I saw you I wanted you more.'

'You said beautiful words to me. I didn't have enough faith in myself to believe them.'

'And now, my love? Now do you believe them?'

'I think so. But why should you even think of me——?'

They wandered around the lake, embracing as they walked. The crickets celebrated their union, and the nightingales blessed it with heavenly music. Leon said, 'Once upon a time——'

'A fairy-story?'

'Maybe. I must practise, for our children.'

'Yes.' She looked across the lake, silvery white in

the early morning before dawn broke. The children—Leon's children. Leon's child already within her, perhaps. The conception of a family, close, loving constantly interacting, needing one another, loving one another. He was the only man in the world she would want like that. 'Tell me the story, Leon.'

'There was a princess once——'

'I know.' She didn't mean to make her voice so harsh. 'I'm sorry. Go on, love.' But she knew that the story of Leon's princess had lurked at the back of her mind, ready to creep out and torment her. 'You loved her very much.' Her recent happiness fell in folds about her feet, like a winding sheet.

His arm tightened around her shoulders. 'I was very young—idealistic. She was beautiful—a picture of loveliness. I dreamed of her nightly, convinced my love was the real thing, and that nothing could stop it.'

The nightingale sang, and Kerrie's heart felt only lovesickness in its song now, not fulfilment. 'Go on—please?'

'I want to tell you everything. Everything I've never had anyone to talk to about before.'

'I hear you.'

'I love you.' He kissed her, but this time she didn't feel the kiss. Leon said in his purring voice, which she had loved forever, but felt now that she was losing, 'I fought my own parents with words, and her parents with constant pleas and recommendations as to my worthiness. One day I managed to meet her alone.'

'Alone?'

'She evaded her maid, the one who had been set to watch her. Oh, yes, it's still the custom in some oriental families. Girls are not credited with making a wise choice of husband.'

'And she confessed her love?'

'We talked for over two hours. Can you imagine, Kerrie? Two hours was all we had to get to know one another. And the more we talked, Kerrie, the more my love faded, like a sensitive flower at noon.'

'Faded?' Kerrie felt a load lift from her soul.

Leon laughed, then, and took her face in his hands. 'I'm sorry, I didn't mean to tease you too much. The story is true, Kerrie. But you will have heard the romantic version, that she was whipped away from me by her mercenary parents, in favour of a prince of royal blood. Sounds good, doesn't it? The truth is a little different. I fell out of love with her as soon as I got to know her. She was narrow, petty. She knew how beautiful her face was, and expected her beauty to buy her the moon. I don't think she'd even thought that one day she would grow old. I don't think she'd ever thought of anyone else but herself in her life. It was a cruel awakening for me, but it made me think. I numbered, there and then, the qualities I would look for in a woman. And, Kerrie, after many years of loneliness, I was beginning to think there was no such woman. I was even beginning to think I should settle for a woman with only skin deep beauty and a medical degree.'

'And?'

'Oh, darling, you want me to say it over and over? I will, because I still can't believe my years of disillusion are over. I met you—on the beach, with very little on! My senses were stirred immediately. It took at least four more hours before I fell head-long, irreversibly in love.'

Kerrie breathed in, confidently. 'I think I feel better now.'

'Is that all? You aren't going to swear undying love for me?'

'Not now. You might get over-confident!' But she kissed him very sweetly all the same, and the kiss took a long time. Then she said, her cheek against his, 'I want to know if the princess really married a handsome prince. Isn't that what all fairy stories are about?'

Leon laughed. 'She married a spoiled overweight prince, yes. Rich—but spot the brain-cell! I'd given him some karate lessons once. If he'd kept it up, he might have kept his figure, but he was too fond of chocolate.'

'You are smug, aren't you?'

'I am.' He stopped again to hold her close. 'You know, I know now what that chap was doing in the film, singing and dancing in the rain! My happiness is threatening to lift us off into orbit.'

'Mine too.' Kerrie looked into his eyes, and stroked his cheek. 'Leon, is there anything at all that would persuade you to take Rick back into the Sultan?'

He smiled, teasing. 'What will you give me?'

'Anything that's mine. I think he's had a lesson he won't forget.'

'Your wish is my command.'

'You're not a genie. Are you?'

'No—fair enough. But I've already told my secretary to make sure Rick knows he can come back if he wants.'

'I love you, Leon. My heart hurts with love. Shall I swear undying love now?'

'Be my guest.'

'I'll miss you very much when you go to Europe, you know.'

'No, you won't—you're coming with me. It's going to be our honeymoon—and we can call in on Brighton too. You wouldn't want me to go there alone?'

'Not anywhere alone. Never alone again.' The moon glowed through the palm fronds, and the crickets sang. Kerrie murmured, 'Let's go back to bed.' And the trees whispered their approval.